MERCILESS

Fated Mates – Book Four

Lilli Carlisle

ALSO BY LILLI CARLISLE

FATED MATES

Tigress

Huntress

Speechless

THE BLACK RIDGE WOLF PACK

Omega's Choice

Ceva's Chance

Karli's Resolve

Laura's Legacy

Lili's Trust

Katrina's Destiny

www.BOROUGHSPUBLISHINGGROUP.com

MERCILESS
Copyright © 2020 LILLI CARLISLE

ISBN 978-1-951055-67-7

4

This has been possible only with the love and support of my family.
Love you Craig, Samantha, Katie, and Jason.

MERCILESS

Chapter One

Marie knew what she was doing was wrong. She'd tried to talk herself out of it, force herself to see reason, anything to stop herself from sitting exactly where she currently was. No surprise when her heart rate sped up. It always happened. Her palms were sweaty, and she rubbed them on her jeans before turning the page on a book she wasn't reading.

Her reusable water bottle was already empty, and there were at least thirty minutes left if he stayed on the same routine. She didn't want to risk running to fill up her bottle, not wanting to miss anything. Marie wasn't the only one who came here, but she was the only one with a legitimate reason. She'd been assigned to do this, sit and watch.

Muscles flexed and strained under the weight being lifted, but they never faltered. Beads of sweat rolled down delicious tanned skin making her almost moan at the sight. She knew from the moment she set her eyes on him that she'd be in a whole new world of trouble, and this time Rose won't be able to save her.

But did Marie look away? Of course not.

Instead, every day from ten in the morning until noon, she sat spellbound while trying to appear unaffected while Texas State Trooper Ben Brown worked out in the large, fully equipped gym installed on the tenth level.

Of course, they required an extensive, plus-sized gym for shifters trapped underground who were unable to go for a run outdoors to burn off any pent-up energy or aggression. They were bears. Aggression was in their DNA.

The Trooper was a human-shifter hybrid who seemed to enjoy the benefits of a good workout. As did Marie for entirely different reasons.

To the left, she noticed two female wolf-shifters were scanning the room. One shook her head and waved off whatever the other wolf had said before leaving the gym. The one who remained removed her T-shirt, and stood preening in her sports bra. It didn't take a rocket scientist to figure out what she had in mind.

Marie watched as the she-wolf stepped onto an elliptical machine directly in front of where Ben was doing leg presses. The she-wolf's outfit didn't cover much, and although.nudity wasn't a big deal for shifters, Ben was mostly human, which meant the woman might as well have been wearing a sign on her barely covered ass, declaring herself available.

Marie almost groaned out loud when the wolf's ass cheeks bounced from under her minuscule shorts. Seriously? Such an obvious ploy to attrack Ben's attention. If that was what it took, Marie was destined to be alone because there was no way in a million years she'd wear that outfit.

Ben didn't appear to notice the bouncy she-wolf and moved on to the dumbbells. Marie had to give the woman credit: she wasn't easily deterred, and moved over to the treadmill across from the mirror Ben was using to check his form, which was on point and drool worthy.

She flipped another unread page with a bit more force than necessary, ripping the page out of the book, and then looked again at her empty water bottle. It didn't matter how thirsty she was, she wasn't going anywhere.

When the she-wolf lowered the zipper on the front of her sports bra, Marie was surprised the shifter's breasts didn't tumble out, and Marie's bear growled and pawed at her to do something about the exhibitionist.

The display reconfirmed that if this was what it took to get a male's attention, Marie would rather be alone. She was a bear-shifter, which made her taller and more substantial than a lot of other female shifter species. Her arms and torso were defined, and she had long muscular legs. Her breasts weren't voluptuous, but they had enough heft to fill out her sweaters. Her body type did not say soft and curvy, or lithe and svelte.

Before she could get any further into unflattering body comparisons, the she-wolf drew her attention. The wolf-shifter was so busy adjusting her bra strap, she didn't notice her bottle of water teetering on the edge of the elliptical machine's handrail. The bottle fell onto the belt, making the shifter misstep, and she went flying off the end of the machine like a torpedo launched from a submarine.

Marie couldn't help but laugh until Ben went over to help the she-wolf to her feet. When he tried to pull his hand out of hers, the shifter refused to let it go as she smiled coyly and brushed her breasts up against his muscled and tattooed arm.

Disgusted, Marie was about to look away when a new problem walked in. A male wolf growled and bunched his shoulders as he approached Ben. Marie was up and out of her chair, intending to head off the impending disaster, but by the time she made it over to Ben, an argument had already erupted, which had the she-wolf gloating from the attention she clearly wanted.

"How dare you touch one of our women," the male bellowed and aggressively puffed out his chest.

"You know, women aren't your or anyone's property. Chill, bro. I was only helping her up after she fell," Ben stated calmly. He turned back to the rack of dumbbells, and Marie knew what would happen next. As the she-wolf's smile widened, the male wolf raised his arm to sucker punch Ben in the back of his head. Before he could get off a blow, Marie reached out, grabbed the male's arm, and flipped him over her back and onto the floor. Ben turned around at the same time Marie jammed her elbow into the wolf's jaw, ending the guy's attempts at getting back up.

There were benefits to being a bear-shifter. One was being stronger than most other shifter breeds.

Unfortunately, there were also drawbacks, and the way Ben was looking at her in that moment was one of them. She wasn't dainty or delicate.

"Time to go," Marie said to Ben, before turning to the wolves. "You two know the rules. The humans are not to be touched. Now leave, or I will be forced to report you to your alpha triad."

"Figures you'd protect him. Humans are bloodthirsty killers. Only a traitor would side with them over shifters." Sure, the nasty comment hurt—every time she heard one it hurt—but she'd never show the effect it had on her.

"And you're the poster boy for *Puppy Weekly*. Now leave," Marie ordered, while extending her six-inch claws for good measure, "before I change my mind and show you the door personally."

As the wolves began walking away, Marie glanced over at Ben to find him staring at her hands.

Her heart fell, and she retracted her claws.

Yep, she was not soft and delicate.

She was a bear.

Chapter Two

"I volunteer," Marie hollered after Mason announced yet another mission to the surface.

For centuries, since the beginning of the industrial age, the veil between the world they lived in and the scorched realm thinned, and was finally broken, allowing the most heinous of creatures, Collector Demons, to roam the Earth again. They stole the souls and bodies of humans, their intent to take over the planet while subjugating all sentient species.

Shifters had spent those centuries destroying the rogue demons and keeping their existence hidden from the humans. However, recently, the Collectors had found a way to repel the tools and magic the shifters had used to keep the attemped annilhilation under control. The entire shifter community knew the world was being overtaken, and there seemed to be no way to stop it from happening.

Before being forced into hiding, ancient goddesses began to bestow their powers upon a select few among the shifter community. Marie's clan had encountered human-shifter hybrids who had some latent powers of their own that they didn't know how to tap into yet. All shifters were tasked with rescuing as many hybrids as they could and bringing them into the relative safety of the shifter world.

Marie's clan, and the North Woods pack, had been underground for nearly a month, the only contact with the outside world was through CCTV video and a network of shifter run communications. The clan and the pack had gone underground into their maze of bunkers when the Collector Demons began sweeping over the surface like a deadly plague. By reports, the situation topside was getting worse by the day.

Collector Demons could easily possess most humans. Turning their souls to dust and leaving bloodthirsty beasts in their wake. The same thing had occurred hundreds of centuries ago, and humans and shifters had united to drive the Collectors back.

Somehow, through the annuls of time, humans turned on the shifter world and human hunters made sport of killing shifter kind. Those who didn't hunt them believed them to be nothing more than fairy tales and movie-created characters, their joined history dismissed as ancient rhetoric or magical thinking typical of unsophisticated societies.

In present day, humankind had no idea that the person standing next to them could be one of the many shifter breeds. There would be no union between their two worlds this time around. Shifters were on their own to protect themselves and fix this, or there'd be no world left for them to live in.

One of the many advantages to being a shifter was that the Collectors couldn't possess them due to their animal half. The discovery of immune human-shifters confirmed that something in their animal DNA protected them, at least from the possession. Any one of the demon-filled bodies dragging themselves around up there could still kill the hybrids.

That was why the god, Ra, had ordered them to track down as many human-shifters as they could and protect them. Between the catastrophic loss of friends, family, homes, and all vestiges of their former lives, and then being forced to have human hybrids among them, their shelter was a powder keg ready to blow.

Many shifters had lost loved ones to the human hunters over the years, blinding them to the fact that not all humans killed shifters, and that the hybrids carried half-shifter DNA.

The first three rescues had taken place in London. Ben, a hybrid, who Marie was charged to watch over, and two human children, Jenny and Matthew, both too young and innocent to be possessed by the Demons. Now that they were underground and under shifter protection, Collectors wouldn't be able to reach them as they grew.

The presence of human children threw the whole nature over nurture argument on its head. No one was born evil. Marie hoped that by the time the children hit puberty, the demons would be eradicated, or at least pushed back behind the veil of mist separating their two worlds. And in that time, two humans who had been raised and protected by shifters would know the truth of their existence and the extent of their love and connection. Change started one person at a time.

Marie began suiting up and arming herself yet again. Once a Collector had taken a human host over, that person ceased to be, and the only way to stop what was left was by inflicting enough damage to their human shells, or by cutting off their heads and forcing the demon to leave. The goddesses had the power to capture them in their mist forms and destroy them.

There was one unusual change among the hosts that hadn't escaped notice: now, some of the Collectors were able to mimic human interaction and thought. Before, though the demons were highly intelligent, they couldn't use a human to their full potential. They'd decompose too quickly and become useless. Now they were, for lack of a better word, longer preserved in their human state.

Today's team consisted of John, the bear clan's general, and Zahra his mate, along with a contingent of bear and wolf-shifters in both animal and human forms. Marie checked her M16 rifle and strapped her sword to her back. The last thing she needed was for her gun to jam in the middle of a firefight. Even though she had the option of turning furry at any time to defend herself, opposable thumbs came in handy when using a gun in longer-range battles.

Matriarch Rose walked across the room with her bright white-blonde hair glowing in the overhead lighting, heading in Marie's direction. Rose had saved Marie's life more than once. The first time when she'd challenged Rose for her position as matriarch of the clan. Her family had forced Marie to undertake a battle she'd wanted no part in, and when she'd lost, Marie had welcomed the chance to surrender her life, such as it was, as a dishonored bear.

However, Rose chose to spare her, but the matriarch's kindness was not shared by most of the clan or the neighboring pack. Marie was branded a traitor, and she did nothing to dispel the accusations. Explanations of her family's control over her would fall on deaf ears, and, more to the point, Marie felt ashamed and guilty for not having defied them, even if it had meant certain death. She questioned her honor ever day since the challenge and came up short.

The second save followed on the heels of the first, when Rose decided not to send Marie back to her family, who would have killed her slowly and painfully after losing.

As it turned out, it was later discovered that Marie's mother, father, and brother had worked alongside the human hunters to eliminate the former alpha triad. Mason and Riker's parents had been ambushed and killed due to Marie's family's lust for power.

Her former relatives were no longer a concern, and the house of horrors she'd grown up in had been bulldozed to the ground. Her basement cell included. But the memories of what she'd endured still haunted her dreams.

Marie wasn't merely a dishonored bear. She was lumped into her family's machinations and schemes even though her alphas knew she had nothing to do with their plotting.

"You're going to the surface again?" Rose asked as she came to stand beside her. "Isn't this the third time in the past week?"

Marie thought for a moment and then said, "Three times sounds about right."

"You don't have to go on every mission that comes up," Rose advised. "You need to rest and let others take over the responsibility of guarding Zahra as she searches for more human-shifters."

"Zahra and John go on every mission. Why should I be any different?"

"Because Zahra is a goddess and an Eye of Ra. As for John, no one would be able to keep him from accompanying his mate into possible danger."

"As long as they go out, so will I. It's my duty to serve this clan." Rose didn't look convinced.

Thankfully, Marie was called to assemble with the others so that Zahra could teleport them all to the site where she believed another human-shifter was hiding.

"I'm okay, Rose," Marie explained. "There's nothing to worry about. I'm a big bear." She flexed her arms. "I can easily swat the bad guys out of my way."

The corners of the matriarch's lips quirked upward as Marie had hoped. "If it weren't for this meeting with the skulk of fox-shifters that arrived earlier today, I would be going along as well."

Marie smiled, knowing Rose would have preferred to have been by Marie's side. The matriarch never backed out of a battle. In truth, she was typically leading the way into the fire.

"How can you guys even trust her?" The question was whispered, but damn advanced shifter hearing made whispering pointless. Marie turned to find a wolf-shifter staring her down with his top lip curled back in disgust.

Rose looked ready to kill, her goddess markings began to glow, and she took a few steps toward the man, essentially wiping the glare off his face. However, she stopped when Marie placed her hand on her friend's shoulder.

"It's okay, Matriarch," she said. "He speaks the truth. Many find it hard to trust me after what I've done."

"No, it's not the whole truth. There were circumstances beyond your control, and I'll be damned if I'll stand by as they question your loyalties. You've proven your worth time and again."

"Please," Marie begged. "Let it go." The last thing she needed was for Rose to go around beating up shifters who found Marie's participation in the clan dubious and distasteful.

With a loud huff and a mean side-eye at the man who'd made the comment, Rose backed away. "Okay, this time. But next time, I'm going to fry him." Sparks flew from the tips of her fingers, reminding everyone that she was a reincarnated goddess as well as the clan matriarch.

Since the first few attacks by the Collectors began, ancient warrior goddesses had been reincarnating all around Marie. Raz, the wolf matriarch, who happened to be a tigress, and Rose, the bear clan matriarch, who happened to be a wolf, along with Zahra, a wolf but not matriarch of any group, all had been embued with the powers of a goddess.

Marie laughed. "Don't fry too many, we still need them." She loved her friend for standing up for her.

"Everyone prepared?" Zahra's words rang out even though she had no voice, her vocal cords having been severed long ago. Thankfully, due in part to her becoming a goddess of Ra, she could be heard without physically speaking or even moving her lips.

Yeah, everything was crazy different, and there was no sign of these changes abating anytime soon. Marie found it was best not to think too hard on the technicalities of it all and accept the weird stuff that kept happening on a daily basis.

Rose walked away, and Marie joined the others by placing her hand on Zahra's shoulder. They were friends. Zahra had shown her kindness, and Marie would protect her. As the room began to fade away, she noticed Ben coming to stand in the doorway.

Moments later they were gone.

***

Ben watched as the group of shifters dematerialized? disappeared? vaporized? to hunt for yet another human-shifter to save. He'd been here for over a month, and all the crazy shit happening around him was beginning to feel normal. He wondered what that said about him.

People popping in and out in various shapes and species, possessing powers beyond imagination. It wasn't the shifter thing that made him jump, it was all the *magic* floating around in the bunkers. It left a prickly sensation across his skin, or at least that's what he'd attributed the weird feeling to. Since arriving, his body seemed to be reacting to everything around it in a way he'd never experienced.

He noticed Marie went on quite a few missions and wanted to know why. "Pardon me, Matriarch. Do you need more people to volunteer to go to the surface?"

"No, we've had many, but thank you for offering, and please call me Rose." What odd turns his life had taken. These people had kidnapped him and forced him to live underground with them. It didn't take long to recognize they meant to help and protect him, and the leaders were actually decent, and treated him with respect.

"Thank you, Rose. One of the reasons I ask is that I saw Marie going along again. Couldn't someone else have taken her place?" He'd been in law enforcement for years. He knew each time anyone went out on a dangerous mission it increased their odds of injury or not making it back.

Rose looked at him with undisguised curiosity. "She volunteers. I can't stop her from what she believes is her duty. Why do you ask?"

Shit. Busted. "Umm, I'm worried. Marie seems to be working herself to the point of exhaustion. It's almost as if she were trying to prove herself every time she goes."

"Sadly, in some ways she is," Rose replied. "But that isn't my story to tell. Can I help you with anything else?"

Ben shook his head as he said, "No. Thank you for your time."

Once she'd turned away, Ben headed back in the direction from which he came. Through endless hallways and multiple stairways, he'd certainly have gotten lost by now if it weren't for his instincts.

Yes, his instincts. Ben had always known he was different. Bigger, faster, and stronger than all his friends throughout school. His reaction time surpassed adults when he was only four years old. However, it wasn't until his eighteenth birthday that he found out why.

He'd had a great childhood. Endless sunny days fishing, followed by evening camp fires under the stars. Ben had done more living outside then in. Summer nights playing baseball with his friends were customarily followed by barbecues. Normal, everyday life that now felt more like fiction than reality.

He clearly remembered the day he'd learned his truth, right down to the music that was playing on the radio. Creedence Clearwater Revival's "Proud Mary" blasted out of the speaker like a birthday anthem. His mom loved old rock bands, and he'd inherited that love. At eighteen, he learned that wasn't all he'd inherited.

They'd done the obligatory homemade cake with candles, and his mom had sung to him before he blew out the candles and made his wish. Whatever he'd wished for, it was nothing compared to what he'd learned that evening.

Ben had been hanging out in his bedroom waiting for his friends to call to let him know when they were picking him up when his mom had called him into the living room. He had been annoyed by the interruption, watching his music videos back before DVRs and subscription TV. Sometimes he'd have to wait all day for his favorite music video to come on again.

When he'd finally pulled his lazy ass out of bed and walked into the living room, he found his mother standing naked in the center of the worn area rug between their two recliners. Before he'd had a chance to ask her if she'd lost her mind, she'd transformed into a full-sized grizzly bear. It had happened so quickly that he blinked a couple times to make sure he was actually seeing what his brain told him was real.

Ben had no idea how long he stood frozen to the spot, but it had to have been at least a minute because his mother had slowly inched closer to him. He watched every move the bear made. At first, he felt scared shitless. Who wouldn't? Once the shock wore off, he took a good look at the beast and realized the bear's brown eyes were familiar. Unbelievably, his mom was staring back at him from that thick furry head. Hestitantly, he reached out and laid his hand on her ruff, and she closed her eyes and let out a chuff that sounded like a sigh.

When she got up on her back legs—she stood over seven feet—he turned, instinctually knowing she was going to change back to human.

After he heard the last rustle of clothing, he turned to see his mom, zipping up her jeans.

"Sit." She motioned to the chair across from the sofa where she planted herself. "Jolting, huh?" He rolled his eyes, and she grinned. "I didn't mean to scare you, but it seemed the most effective way of telling you so you'd believe me."

"Mission accomplished."

"I can't give you a shifter species history since there's more lore than facts about the first shifters, but suffice it to say, we've been around as long as there has been humans."

"I'm guessing you're not all bears."

She smiled. "No. Mostly predatory animals."

"Natch." He looked down at his body, then back at her before he asked, "Can I do that?"

She shook her head. "Unfortunately, no. You're half shifter with more human DNA than shifter, which prevents you from changing form. But, my son, there's so much you can do, and there's a whole other world you need to learn."

There was a lot of explaining after her big reveal, and now, Ben was discovering how much of what she'd told him was fact, and then some.

He rubbed his tired eyes, willing the memories back before he sunk too deep. His mother had to be alive, even if he couldn't reach her. According to these people, shifters were immune to the Collectors, making his half-shifter blood a boon in this war. His preference was to be able to shift into a bear like his mom. Other than his enhanced abilities, he knew he was as close to becoming a shifter as he was ever going to be.

"Ben. Ben," a happy voice called to him from the playroom in the section of the facility set aside for the humans and human-shifters. The area was laid out in a circle with doors to each person's private space, size determined by the number of family members inhabiting the rooms.

At the center of their little community was a courtyard with a well-stocked playroom and lounge with couches and chairs, along with movies and gaming systems. Their hosts had thought of every form of entertainment available since there weren't television stations or streaming channels since the war began. All traditional forms of communication had ceased when the Collectors infected a significant portion of the human population.

Jenny and Matthew came running up to him, their tiny hands covered in bright paint. They each wore a smock, but by the looks of the two of them, the purpose of the protective covering had failed completely.

Smiling faces were precisely what he needed. "We made you a picture to hang up in your room," Jenny said, before wrapping her arms around his right leg, followed by Matthew on his left.

Ben could feel their squishy paint-covered fingers all the way through his jeans. "Wow, a picture. I need a picture to brighten it up in there. How'd you know?"

Jenny's smile was wide and her eyes twinkled. She spoke for the two of them. "I'll never tell. It's a secret."

His jeans clung to their hands briefly as the two children pulled away. Matthew even took the time to wipe the back of his hands on Ben's knee before running toward the easel. Oh, to be a five-year-old again.

He'd found Matthew hiding on a double-decker bus in London. The poor little guy hadn't spoken a word since, but thankfully he'd had a name tag on, so at least they knew what to call him. Ben figured Matthew had been on a school trip with his class when things began falling apart around them.

Ben hadn't dwelled on where the other children might be. He couldn't have saved them all, but damned if he hadn't tried to find as many as possible. The guilt had been crushing, and every time he looked at these two sweet souls, he felt a lance through his heart at all the children who weren't saved.

As the kids led the way, he made sure not to get his painted pants to close to any of the furniture. Hope, a bear-shifter, had been taking care of the kids since they'd arrived. She smiled at him from the table where she was busy cutting up carrots. He'd been told there was a hydroponic growing facility down here somewhere, so they didn't have to go without fresh fruits and vegetables during their time underground. But he wondered, even with all their preparations, how long could the food and water last. This war didn't look like it was going to end anytime soon.

It wasn't too often the shifters showed him any emotion other than anger and distain. However, there were a few who had been kind and welcoming. Marie was among them.

"Sorry about your jeans," Hope said with a grimace. "But the paint is water based, so it'll come out." Her shoulders raised in a shrug. "Maybe."

He looked down at his newly designed jeans. Stripes of yellow and smudges of red, blue, and brown made for a throwback sixties hippy look. "No worries. If it doesn't, at least they're unique."

Hope looked at him as if he was one brick short of a load. "Unique, yeah. That's what we'll call it."

"Look, look," Jenny cried. "We painted it together."

Ben stepped around a pile of plush stuffed bears—why did the animal choice not surprise him—and took a look at their masterpiece. "Oh, wow. That's, umm, great work guys." He wasn't too sure what he was looking at. In the center of the page was an oversized round head with red hair and green eyes. At first, he thought it was a picture of Matthew until Jenny clarified.

"That's you," she explained. "And those are all the bad people."

Ben noticed the black figures creeping along the edges of the paper. He understood that these two had been through severe trauma and had to work it out any way they could. "What am I doing?" As far as he could tell, he was holding a frying pan.

"You're fighting them off like you did when you found us. See," Jenny said as she pointed toward the bottom of the paper. "That's Matthew and me hiding under the couch."

He remembered that couch. It had been in the cottage where he'd taken the kids to hide from the Collectors. That was where the shifters had found them.

Going to his knees in front of them, Ben had to make sure they knew they were being protected. "Both of you are safe here. Everyone is going to do everything they can to make sure nothing hurts you or Matthew."

Both looked at him with big, trusting eyes. "We know. The bad guys'll get their bums kicked."

Ben looked from the kids to Hope, looking for an explanation for the bum-kicking comment. She shook her head, looking as confused as he felt.

"Jenny, you are absolutely right," Ben agreed. "Where did you hear the term bum-kicking?" For all he knew, it could've come from her parents before the world went insane.

"Marie," she answered readily. "See, she's right there." She touched the painting. "The big bear."

Ben looked to where Jenny was pointing, and could make out a big brown oval with pink streaks for claws and one hell of a pair of shiny white canine teeth. Marie would have been impressed.

"Okay, children, it's time to clean up before dinner," Hope said as she stood and came to stand beside him. "Off to the sinks with those gooey hands, and use the soap this time."

"Okay," Jenny answered. "Don't forget your painting, Ben."

"I won't, sweetheart. Thank you, both of you, for giving me such an amazing gift." This time Matthew's smile reached his eyes. That wasn't always the case, and Ben would take it as a good sign.

"Well, they are creative little munchkins." Hope chuckled. "They're wonderful."

"And you're wonderful for taking care of them so well," Ben said. "Thank you."

Hope looked him up and down before saying, "You're different from most of the other humans I've met."

"Half shifter might have something to do with it." Ben went with an easy answer. He'd had enough of being singled out since he'd arrived here.

"No, it's not that," she said but didn't elaborate. "Be sure to take your painting with you when you leave."

Hope turned away, but Ben remembered one more thing he'd wanted to ask. "Hey. Do you know how often Marie comes to visit the kids?"

She turned around to look at him. "Usually, every day, that is if she isn't out on a mission." Hope waved her hand over toward the toy-filled corner. "She's responsible for most of this."

Ben looked at the stack of toys overflowing from a plastic tub that was being used as a stand-in for a toy box. "Where is she getting them?"

"As far as I know, on missions," Hope replied. "She's always bringing the kids one thing or another back from the surface."

"Thank you," Ben said. He unclipped his still-wet gift from the easel and carried it, at arm's length, back to his room on the other side of the courtyard.

Once there, he took the painting to his efficiency kitchen and used the three magnets he'd found in one of the kitchen drawers to secure it to the front of his full-size fridge. Hanging from the cupboard alongside it was his silver Texas State Trooper badge. Years of hard work and sacrifice for a shiny piece of metal that no longer meant a thing. He didn't dwell on that too long. It was best to stay in the moment, considering the past had been washed away in a sea of blood.

Ben stood admiring the kids' artwork a few more moments, with most of his attention on the brown oval fighting by his side. There was something about Marie that drew him like no one else, but he couldn't put his finger on it.

Of course, she was gorgeous with her dark hair and eyes, but her looks weren't why he felt a pull, a connection, hell, he couldn't put it into words, but somehow he felt connected to her. Since the first moment he'd laid eyes on her and took in her scent in the cottage, he was hooked. His mom had taught him how to control some of his more aggressive inherited traits, but in that moment, Ben would have lost control if Marie hadn't moved out of his sight line when she did.

His urge to take her where she stood had been overwhelming.

He slid out of his newly painted jeans and laid them over the shower rod in the bathroom. He'd have to wash them later because he had more important things on his mind. Dressed only in his boxer briefs and a T-shirt, Ben sat on his couch and pulled the laptop sitting on his metal coffee table closer to him. He'd been given the device by the shifter leaders, which strengthened his belief he wasn't a prisoner, as the leaders had explained. It seemed they were all in this together.

Ben spent the next few hours continuing his search for any sign of his mother. The laptop allowed him access to video feeds from all over the world that had been set up and provided by shifters. The shifters here had done the same in this area.

There had to be a way to find out which one of these was the closest to Lufkin, Texas. He had a good idea where his mother would be hiding, waiting for the worst to pass. Ben needed to figure out a way of getting there and bringing her back here, which might be a bigger challenge than he was capable of accomplishing.

"I'll find you, Mom, I promise," he whispered and touched his fingers to the screen of video feed from the Houston area.

Chapter Three

The moment her boots hit the hot pavement, Marie knew they were being watched. Collectors, shifters, or humans, that still remained to be seen, but she wasn't taking any chances and moved closer to Zahra. John was using his body to shield Zahra from the other side.

"Seriously, you two," Zahra growled. *"I'm a goddess of Ra. I can take care of myself."*

Marie didn't take her eyes off the houses surrounding them. They appeared to be in a retirement community in Florida, given the Miami Dolphins flags she could see hanging off various porches. It did make her wonder, though, if the human-shifter they were here to find was elderly. She was prepared to carry them if they were.

"Mate, it is in my nature to protect you," John explained to Zahra. "I could no more stop myself from this as stop the sun from setting."

"Don't get all eloquent with me, big guy," Zahra laughed. *"We'll deal with your nature later."*

She turned to Marie. *"And what's your excuse."*

"I live to be a pain in your ass," Marie deadpanned.

"You guys are incorrigible. Let's find the human-shifter and get the hell out of here. This place is giving me the creeps." Zahra wrapped her arms around her waist as she looked around.

Marie had to agree. Between the blood-stained walker standing in the middle of the street, and the personal oxygen canister lying on the grass, this place was a nightmare waiting to happen. In several locations, the odd decomposing hand, arm, and what appeared to be torso lay in brown pools of dried blood while other dark stains in the area had been picked clean.

A lone golden retriever sat on a porch five doors down, as if waiting for his owners to come home. It wagged its bushy tail upon seeing their group approach. The sight struck a chord deep inside of Marie, and for a moment the sight of his loneliness was all she could concentrate on. If she had the chance, she'd take the dog back to Jenny and Matthew to love on. Marie couldn't bring herself to leave it out here.

"I want to bring that dog back for the human kids," Marie said. "They need a pet, and the dog needs a home."

Zahra looked up at Marie, and for a moment she thought her friend would argue, but thankfully not. *"Okay."*

They moved out together following the directions Zahra gave. Systematically, Marie scanned the area watching for any signs of movement. The odd pet cat wandered out looking for attention, but nothing more. She was beginning to think that her senses were wrong, then she heard the unmistakable click of the cylinder rotating in a handgun seconds before the gunfire started ringing out.

John grabbed Zahra around her waist and ran for one of the parked cars ahead of them, while Marie covered them both from behind and returned fire every few seconds. She felt fire race through her, but she didn't have the time to stop and inspect the bullet that was now lodged in her side.

The team found cover behind parked cars, and both sides ceased fire. Marie kept watch as Zahra and John discussed their plan of attack, but only after the general assured himself Zahra didn't have a scratch on her. That familiar melancholy feeling rose inside of Marie, but she tamped it down hard. Across the lawn, a falcon-shifter was in the process of taking off his clothes before changing into his agile and swift bird.

Each shifter from their combined bunkers had a link to one another due to the two alpha triads' connection, and the exchange of a drop of each of their blood. The falcon flew around to the back of the house from where the shots were fired to get a better look.

"I can only see one human. She's barricaded herself on the top floor of the house," he reported. *"I'm perched on a small deck outside her window. She's looking at me. Holy shit, the human tried to shoo me away, saying that a bird as pretty as me shouldn't stay around here. I like her already."*

"Is that the human-shifter you're looking for, Zahra?" John asked his mate.

"It would appear to be," she answered with a nod of her head. *"The one trying to kill us."*

"And we can't shoot her, right?" Marie asked for clarification. "Maybe not the organs, but how about a graze or two, to take the wind out of her."

Zahra turned to look at her. *"No, we can't sh—Oh my gods, you've been shot, Marie."*

John turned his head. "It's nothing to worry about. Only a graze." She didn't like being the center of attention for any reason.

"By the blood soaking your vest and pants, it's more than a minor hit," John remarked, with a healthy amount of worry lining his face.

"Let's take care of this extraction. Then when we get everybody back safe and sound into the bunker, I'll let Jewel have a look."

They didn't look convinced, but what else could they do. It wasn't as if the team could get up and leave. They still had a mission to complete, even if the subject seemed to be trying to kill them.

"Well then, I need to try something to speed this along," Zahra said, and her palms began glowing. The golden hue surrounded their group and spread to both sides of the street. *"There we go."* Without warning, the goddess stood up from behind their cover.

A single shot was fired. Marie knew she was the closest to Zahra, so she angled her body in front of her friend, knowing full well that the move would kill her. She waited for the impact and the searing pain that would accompany it, but neither came. John turned to stare at something directly behind Marie.

She moved her body slightly and caught a glimpse of a shiny object at the back of her head. When she turned all the way around, she found the bullet hanging in midair exactly where her head had been.

"Shit, you really would take a bullet for me," Zahra growled. *"Stop that this minute. I will not have you doing that to yourself."*

"Hey. I tried to save your ass, so can we keep the lecture short?" Marie growled back. Adrenaline was coursing through her veins causing her heart to beat faster and her wound to bleed all the more. "I told you I would protect you. That has not changed."

"I see John's not the only one I need to have a talk with," Zahra huffed out.

"Um…guys." Marie looked in the direction of where the wolf-shifters were pointing.

There on the porch of the same house from where the shots were being fired, stood a young woman, maybe in her midtwenties. Her hands were in the air, and she began to walk toward them. The team spread out around her, unsure if she was still a threat.

"Come on. Get it over with," she demanded. "It's obvious I can't fight you."

Zahra looked at Marie and John, unsure of what to say. Marie decided to be blunt. Okay, so maybe it wasn't "decided." She knew herself better than that. She was always blunt, decorum be damned. "Get on with what? You're the one who started shooting at us first."

"The killing. Whatever you call it when you change people. I know that's what you guys do because I'm pretty sure my grandma didn't want to pry open my skull with a melon baller before everything around here blew up," she screeched, the volume and octave increasing as she became more frantic. "Those 'new' people weren't my family or friends, and neither are all of you."

"We're not going to do that," Marie said. "We came here to save you."

The woman's dark eyes went wide when the falcon landed only ten feet in front of her and returned to his human form.

"Thanks for calling me pretty," he said. "I'm rather proud of my falcon form."

The hybrid's eyes went from wide with fear to rolling into the back of her head as she fainted onto the overgrown grass.

"Well, that was a lot easier than I thought it was going to be," John said, before rounding the car and walking toward the unconscious woman.

Zahra followed him, but when Marie took a step forward, her right leg gave out from under her sending her to the ground. No matter how many times she tried to right herself, she couldn't pick her body up. Her friend ran to Marie's side and immediately began applying pressure to her stomach wound.

"We have to get Marie back for medical attention. Join hands," she ordered. *"I will begin trying to heal her on the way."*

"No, grab the dog first," Marie said, as she tried to turn her head in the direction of the last place she'd seen the golden retriever. "For the kids, please."

John disappeared for a few seconds, but was soon back with a happy dog in his arms, licking his face. "Got him, let's go."

It felt surreal to her to be lying flat on her back, looking up into the faces of the team surrounding her. Marie couldn't help but wonder how many of them thought she was better off dead.

The feel of the ground beneath her faded, and so did her consciousness.

Maybe this was the best solution for everyone.

***

Marie growled at the noise. She didn't remember setting her alarm. Its incessant beeping was driving her around the bend. She tried to move her arm to swat at it, but found her arm was too heavy to lift. In fact, her entire body felt heavy and lethargic. She tried to shake it off, but nothing helped and for some reason, she wasn't really concerned by that fact. Odd.

In the distance, she could make out a bright blue light even though she was positive her eyelids were closed. How was she not finding this worrisome? The light grew larger or she was getting closer to it, at the moment she couldn't tell which it was.

It began taking shape, slowly solidifying into the form of a grizzly bear, though still made of blue light. He stood less than twenty feet away from her, staring as if waiting for something to happen. When Marie looked closer, she recognized those green eyes. Ben?

She struggled to move closer to him, but again her body was heavy and cumbersome, refusing to respond and causing her to thrash even harder as the bear began fading. *No.*

"Easy, easy, don't want to knock over the machines," said a deep rich voice with a slight southern twang.

"Ben?"

"Hey there," he replied. "You about done lying around in here?"

Her eyelids flew open. "You heard me?"

"Yes."

"How?"

"Your triad."

"Why?"

"Are we down to one-word sentences again? I'd hoped our conversations had passed that stage long ago." He grinned in his usual sexy way, making her wish for things she could never have.

"Ah, I see our patient is awake," Jewel said as she came up to the side of her bed. "How do you feel?" Marie barely stopped herself from saying *like I've been shot.*

Instead, she began internally cataloging her aches and pains and found nothing she couldn't tolerate. "I'm fine." Marie could take the pain. She'd had a lot of experience with various forms of it.

Jewel's eyebrows rose high onto her forehead, and the corner of her lips quirked downward. "Yeah, you expect me to believe that."

"You were shot," Ben said, as if she could have forgotten. Remembering how much blood she'd lost and how her body had given out before Zahra whisked them back to the compound, Marie wondered why wasn't she dead?

"I'm aware of that. I was there at the time," she said gruffly.

"Friggin' bears," he groused. "You never admit when you're hurt and need help."

Marie had to wonder how many bear-shifters he'd met. "How would you know?"

"My mother is a grizzly-bear-shifter."

"Okay. Maybe you have a point of reference." His grin deepened. "You don't have to be so damn smug about it."

"There's the Marie I know." Ben laughed.

Marie growled, making him smile even wider. "What about the dog?" The last thing she remembered was seeing it in the general's arms.

"You'll be happy to know that Jenny and Matthew are doting over him as we speak. He's had a quick checkup to make sure he was healthy, and now he is making himself right at home," Ben said with a strange look on his face. She didn't have time or the patience to figure out what his expression meant. If she wasn't dying, she wanted out of the infirmary.

"Good." At least the dog was safe.

Marie glanced over at one of the other beds in the ward and recognized the woman who'd shot her. "How's the human-shifter? My would-be assassin."

"Still unconscious," Ben advised. "Jewel's been running tests to make sure she's okay before being moved to her own room."

"Can I get in a word around here? I'm only the doctor," Jewel asked while placing her hands on her hips.

"Sorry," Ben and Marie responded in unison.

"Okay then, one thing at a time. Marie, the bullet punctured your pancreas and one of your kidneys. If you were anything but a shifter, you'd be dead. Raz, Rose, and Zahra have spent a substantial amount of time healing you to get you to this point, which is better than dead, but nowhere near ready to leave my infirmary." Marie growled again. Jewel ignored her. "Second, we'll need to track your lineage, Ben, to find out which clan you're family hails from."

Dead. The word floated around her mind, and part of her wondered what had made them try so hard. "Excuse me, what do you mean by 'this point'? Aren't I healed?" Sure she was in pain, but that wasn't new.

"Well, you're not going to bleed out and die, if that's what you're asking." Jewel shook her head and tapped something onto her tablet. "Now that I have your attention let's have a look to see how your wound is healing."

Jewel set her tablet down, pulled on a pair of gloves, and moved Marie's blanket to the side while ensuring that only her bandaged abdomen was visible. Marie watched as layers of blood-stained gauze and tape were removed, revealing…nothing? *What the…*

"What the…?" Ben stood to get a better look at her stomach. "I saw that wound when you came in six hours ago, there was extensive damage."

"Maybe the goddesses are getting better with their healing abilities," Marie suggested. "Since that's all fixed, if you don't mind, I'll be on my way." She grabbed the bed rail and attempted to sit up, but was soon lying back down and crying out in pain. "Shit, what now?" She clutched at her side as flames licked at her stomach.

"The alpha triads are on their way, along with Zahra and John. We'll figure this out," Jewel explained, before removing the remaining bandages. She grabbed a bottle of saline and washed away the dried blood for a better look.

Marie laid her throbbing head back against her pillow. "It may not look like there's a hole in my side, but it sure as hell feels like it." She shouldn't have moved, but who could blame her for trying to get out of the infirmary. Did anyone actually enjoy being in one of these places?

"Can you give her something for the pain?" Ben asked Jewel. "She's suffering."

"No, I need to stay alert." Marie couldn't afford to be hindered by drugs, it would slow her reaction time. "I'll be fine."

Ben looked down at her. His eyes seemed to become an even deeper shade of green. "I will watch over you, I swear it. Nothing will harm you."

Marie was trying to figure out why Ben was there, and why he took an interest in her well-being. Sure, he seemed like a good guy, but if more than a hundred words had passed between them, she'd be surprised. Another bolt of pain pinned her back onto the bed when she tried to turn to her side. It felt as if hot branding irons were being pressed against her organs.

"Okay," Marie said through gritted teeth. "Give me the good stuff."

Jewel walked away, returning seconds later with a syringe in her hand. Marie was thankful the doctor lined the needle up with a port on her IV line. She didn't want to think about being poked at the moment. The thought alone made her wince, the actual pinch might push her over the edge.

"Why is she in so much pain?" Ben asked. "When she woke up, she wasn't suffering like this."

"I suspect it's from her trying to jump out of her bed to make a break for it," Jewel answered while capping the syringe and dropping it into a yellow container.

Marie watched as Jewel did her work and Ben scowlded. As Marie's pain began to fade, her mind wandered, and she absently wondered if she'd ever caught a scent so enticing. More people joined them. "Welcome to the party folks."

Her medication was taking hold, making her unable to edit her comments before they came flying out of her mouth. Ben seemed amused, and again she thought his presence odd, but welcome.

"Gods, you smell so good," Marie said to Ben, or to the blur where he'd been moments before. Everything was getting a bit fuzzy around the edges. "My bear wants to roll around in it."

All conversation stopped, and she thought something was wrong, but she felt so much better now the silence didn't bother her as she drifted away on a fluffy cloud of painkillers. There would be plenty of time to deal with whatever came up next. Right now, all she wanted to do was to curl into sleep, where her physical and emotional pain no longer existed.

***

Ben watched as Marie fell off into sleep while the room remained silent for a moment longer before Raz, Rose, and Zahra held their glowing palms over Marie's stomach in an attempt to heal her further.

John, the general of the bear clan, walked over to him and said, "Maybe you should wait outside."

Without missing a beat, Ben replied, "You'll have to beat me unconscious for that to happen."

John's head snapped back as he gave him an appraising look. Ben was confident the big bear-shifter was sizing him up to determine the best way to slap him down with those claws.

"He gave his word to watch over her," Jewel explained. "Um…and FYI, Ben's mother is a grizzly-bear-shifter."

"So you've known about shifters for a while," Mason said from across the room. "That's why you weren't shocked about our animal forms."

"To be honest, all the magic has me freaked, but yes, I've known since my mom shifted in front of me when I turned eighteen."

"And your dad?" Raz asked.

"I have no idea who or where he is," Ben answered. "Never met him."

The goddesses were still working on Marie when Ben realized he was holding Marie's hand. He didn't bother letting it go because he wasn't leaving. Some people may not stand by their word. He wasn't one of them.

"He must have been human. Do you mind if I take a sample of your blood?" Jewel asked, her curiosity was written all over her face.

"You didn't while I was knocked unconscious to be brought here?" That was surprising.

"No, we would never to do that without your permission. If we'd had to save your life, then you bet, but Marie didn't knock you over the head too hard," Jewel explained, a touch of amusement in her tone.

"Thanks." Jewel's admission made him feel a better, and put the group in a new light. For the most part, he'd been an outsider, and treated as such. But, they'd been kind and concerned about his well-being, and now he knew they showed him the same respect they had for each other. "You can take as much as you need, but I'm not moving from this spot."

"No problem," Jewel agreed before turning away again.

Ben inched closer to the bed to get a better look at what was happening. Other than a warm yellow glow, he wasn't able to see much. Then Matriarch Rose leaned toward him, without taking her hands away from Marie, and gave him a sniff. Her mates, Mason and Riker, growled softly.

"Can it you two. I was simply checking," she said.

"And?" Mason asked. "Your opinion?"

"Smells normal to me. Nothing special," she advised. "No offense, Ben."

"None took." He hadn't understood Marie's comment to be applied to his personal hygiene, and he didn't wear cologne, so he figured the drugs had loosened her tongue and made her say wacky things. Now, Rose sniffing him and reporting he was "nothing special" had him rethinking Marie's admission. He knew shifters had heightened senses. His were, and he was a hybrid. Huh. Maybe she liked the way he smelled. When she felt better, he'd see if she meant what she said. "How is she?" Since he couldn't see the damage, he had no way to base how the procedure was progressing.

All three women looked up at him, but said nothing. "Are you guys doing that private triad link stuff, 'cause I'd prefer it if you said it out loud, please. Is Marie going to be okay?"

Raz spoke up first. "Yes. A few days of rest and her natural shifter healing will expedite what we are unable to do."

Ben let out a deep breath and sat down in the chair beside Marie's bed, not relinquishing his hold on her hand. He hadn't been grandstanding, someone would have to physically tear him away from her. Even then he'd fight it.

Why he felt so strongly about watching over her, he didn't question. Now was not the time to examine the emotional context of what he was feeling. He was a protector by nature and profession.

Most likely that's all it was.

Chapter Four

"So who wants to be the one to tell them?" Raz asked, and the office went silent. She realized it was odd, everything was weird these days, but she didn't see the problem. "It's not the end of the world."

"In reality, it might be," Riker said while pointing up.

"I meant about Ben," she explained. "Not the Collectors topside."

"Are we sure this is even possible?" Axel asked as he joined her on the couch. "He's human."

Zahra spoke up. *"He's equal parts grizzly and human."*

"But mates?" Mason, the pack alpha, asked. "Neither of them are alpha. How can they be fated?"

"Ahem," John coughed while pointing between himself and Zahra.

"Point taken," Mason muttered.

"I'm not dropping that news at Marie's feet. The poor woman does everything in her power to make up for her past as it is now. Imagine how far she'd go if she knew Ben, who's half human, was her fated mate," Rose stated.

"She would have taken that bullet intended for me," Zahra said, looking pensive. *"Marie seems to have no qualms about sacrificing her life. I understand loyalty, but there's a difference between that and being reckless."*

"Marie hasn't forgiven herself for the past. Instead, she's taken over the responsibility for her whole family, even though she had nothing to do with anything they'd planned," Raz explained. She'd seen the signs every time she ran into Marie, head down, no eye contact unless spoken to, trying not to make the smallest of waves.

"It's not as if members of the clan and pack allow her to forget it," Rose grumbled. "Some of them can be downright vicious in the way they treat her. I almost fried a wolf this morning because of it."

"Did you see Ben's eyes shift when you suggested he step out and leave Marie?" Riker, Rose's mate, and the clan beta asked. "If I didn't know that he couldn't, I would have thought he was about to shift."

"That one caught me by surprise," John answered. "Are we sure he's only half bear?"

"And what about the scent thing. It's how fated mates find each other." Xander, the beta for the wolf pack, brought up an important point. Scent was everything to shifters.

"We have to be wrong," John stated. "There's no way this is possible."

"How about the fact that Marie let me drug her with pain killers only after Ben swore he would stay with her. I doubt she'd trust any of us enough to let her guard down like that," Jewel said.

"This is insane," Zahra growled. *"Oh great God Ra, you there? You gave me the power to find these people, now tell me what to do with them. Is this part of the master plan?"* She waited for a moment. *"It's always about you and when you want to talk, isn't it. Fine, don't answer me. See if I come running the next time you call."*

Raz couldn't help but be amused watching Zahra have an argument with thin air, even though everyone in attendance knew a god was listening.

"Look, I understand everyone's concern and anger toward certain humans." Raz sighed. "I get the hostility. They'd locked me away as a hunting trophy, to be taken out for sport. But we know all humans aren't like that, and I sure don't think the human-shifters are like the hunters. Of course they're scared. We all are about what comes next. Wouldn't alliances with the human-shifters be more beneficial than hate?"

Her mates, Axel and Xander, gathered Raz into their arms. "You always seem to find a way to the heart of the matter, mate. We are blessed to have you and our daughter."

"We have a lot to consider," Mason stated. "There are a lot of variables in this situation."

"Yes, we do," Rose agreed. "Until then, our suspicions remain among us."

***

"Why are you hovering?" Marie asked with a slight growl. "I'm completely capable of walking back to my room all by my big self." She hadn't been able to shake Ben. The man was a bloodhound.

He didn't even break stride. He simply looked down at her. "You were released from the hospital minutes ago. What's wrong with someone caring if you fall over dead?"

"I'm not used to it, and I'm not even close to death, Trooper. So back off before I go all furry on your ass and slice you up," Marie threatened. Did she really want him to go? No. However, he didn't need to know that. No one needed to know that, ever.

"I guess you are feeling better. You haven't lost your surly attitude and sharp tongue," Hope said as they neared the courtyard outside their rooms. Marie had been moved closer to the human-shifters to protect them if anyone thought to take a swipe at one of them in revenge. Whoever tried wouldn't get far and would end up having to deal with her pissed off bear in the bargain.

"Bite me," she grumbled.

"Now, if that's an invitation...?" Ben didn't get a chance to finish that sentence before Jenny and Matthew came running out of their play area with their new dog, whose tail was wagging in high gear. Marie was happy the pup seemed to be fitting in well.

"Marie, Marie...you're back," Jenny cheered while Matthew excitedly waved his stuffed toy in the air. "You were gone so long."

Marie went to her knees and wrapped both kids in her arms while the dog danced around the three of them. It all felt so normal and frightening at the same time. "It was only a few days, guys. You knew I was coming back."

"It was forever," Jenny corrected while holding her arms out wide to emphasize how long it had been.

Marie imagined for small children a couple days may seem like months when they're used to seeing her every day. "How's your new doggie working out?" By the looks of the golden retriever, he'd settled in well and seemed happy.

Matthew quickly ran over and wrapped his arms around the dog's neck, and Jenny answered for them both, as always. "Archie's the best puppy ever."

Unexpectedly, the little girl's big blue eyes filled with tears even as she lauded the dog's worth. Marie gathered Jenny up into her arms and went to join Hope, who was busy cleaning away what looked to be an Archie accident beside one of the couches. Hope and the kids had a larger apartment with two bedrooms, one for her and one for the kids. As they grew, they'd have to add a third bedroom so that each had their own space.

Marie often wondered how Hope felt about being given the children to care for as a young, single bear-shifter, but now wasn't the time to ask as Jenny had broken out into full-blown sniffles.

"Oh dear, what's wrong, peanut?" Hope asked as she threw away the bag with the Archie mess, and then held out her arms to take the little girl.

When Jenny didn't answer, Marie tried to explain. "She was telling me her new dog's name, and then she began to tear up."

Marie handed the child over to Hope, and the three of them sat down on the couch. Ben was keeping Matthew busy so that they could concentrate on Jenny.

"What's wrong?" Hope asked while cuddling the girl close. "You're safe here, you can tell us anything."

Marie's heart was breaking for the little girl whose red cheeks glistened with tears. "You can tell us, sweetie, and if we can fix it, we will."

Jenny looked between the two of them as if deciding how much to say. "My puppy at home was named Archie. I miss him." The child looked up at them as if she'd said something horrible.

"Is that why you used the same name for your new puppy?" Hope asked.

Marie's mind raced with possible ways she could get to Jenny's home to look for her missing dog. She was unsure any of the goddesses would agree to take her to the other end of the bunker system, let alone to the surface. She was still under strict orders to rest.

"Do you know your address, honey? Is that the last place you saw your Archie?" Marie asked, which, of course, got Ben's attention.

He walked over and stood in front of Marie. "You're not cleared to go to the surface until you've taken time to rest and recuperate."

Marie smiled at Jenny before turning away and giving Ben the glare of death, as he'd begun calling it. Apparently, she used it often enough that it deserved a name. In the happiest voice, she could muster at that moment so as not to worry Jenny, she said, "Super

Trooper, I've been resting for days, and it would be good for you to remember that you have no power over me."

Instead of being angry, the damn human-shifter began grinning. "No, I agree. I don't have the power to stop you. However, Jewel does, and she's the one who told you to rest when we left the infirmary."

"And who's going to tell her, you?" Marie asked with a bite in her voice.

"If you force me to." Ben didn't even squirm under her anger. *Why does that make him more appealing?*

"Guys, one issue at a time," Hope cut in. "Was your puppy at home, Jenny?"

It was good to see that Jenny's tears were slowing down. "No. He died in the accident a long time ago."

Shit. Marie admonished herself for bringing the dog to the bunkers. She may have inadvertently reminded Jenny of past pain. Even when she was trying to do good, it blew up in her face.

"What accident," Hope asked.

"The one in the car with Mommy and Daddy," Jenny answered.

This was not what Marie had expected and hated herself all the more for asking the next question. However, to help Jenny, they had to know what they were dealing with. "Honey, do you know where your parents are now?"

"With Archie," she said plainly.

Damn. Jenny's parents must have died in a car accident.

Shit. Ben's voice echoed in Marie's head. She knew he'd been given the ability to hear what was being said in public conversations, but he'd never once spoke through the link.

Wait a minute, I heard you in my head, Marie said, shocked at the connection.

Hmmm, unusual, but helpful. Now's not the time to explore why it's happening. Let's make good use of every tool we have. Ben looked calm. He always looked calm. Did they train for that at the police academy?

Hope was watching the two of them closely, but didn't say a word. Instead, she snuggled Jenny closer while Ben went back to play with Matthew.

"I'm sorry. I wish I could fix that for you," Marie said. Maybe she was entering the on-ramp for the expressway to hell, but she thought, in a way, it was a blessing that the girl's parents had died before Jenny was forced to witness them being taken over by Collector Demons. Marie knew full well that hell existed, or rather Hades, but it was nothing remotely close to what humans had described the place as being. There was no fire and brimstone to be found. In fact, it never reached above seventy-six degrees there. The torture though…Dwelling on those thoughts right now was not productive. Marie had to get her head on straight.

"It's okay. Sometimes I get sad," Jenny admitted as she fought back a yawn.

"I think it's time for a little downtime and maybe a nap," Hope said before standing with Jenny in her arms. "Matthew, honey, it's time for your nap."

Matthew looked up at Ben, as if begging him to let him stay and play. "Sorry, buddy, around here, Hope's the boss. She knows what's best for you."

The scowl Matthew pulled off was impressive. Marie had to give him props for that. He threw his stuffed bear onto the ground before storming off toward their rooms.

Ben came over and sat next to Marie on the couch in the play area. "You know, I'm actually happy to see the little guy has a bit of a temper."

"Agreed. Anything but that lost look." Every time Marie saw one of the kids gazing off into space, their lips quivering, the eyes filled with dread, it shredded her heart and brought back memories she needed to keep a handle on.

"Yeah, and it shows he's getting more comfortable with his surroundings," Ben said. "See, we can agree on things."

Before she could come up with a fitting reply, the newly arrived human-shifter poked her head out of her room and scanned the area. Marie had forgotten about the woman, what with everything else going on around her. The hybrid didn't look any worse for the wear. In fact, she didn't have a scratch on her.

"How does she fit in?" Marie asked.

"Actually, this is the first time I've seen her since she was in the infirmary after you guys came back. I've been otherwise occupied." Ben smirked, causing her to growl. *How is it that he seems to have sway over my emotions? Who invited him?*

"I didn't ask you to hang around the infirmary with me." Though she'd enjoyed it.

"Somebody had to or you would've taken off the moment Jewel turned her back."

Whether he was correct was not the point. He had no authority over her. He had no say about what she did and with whom, and he damn well better keep his nose out of her business.

"Do we know her name?"

"You didn't even try to conceal your change of subject." Ben laughed and shook his head. "I think someone mentioned her name is Raine."

"Someone mentioned it was going to rain?" Marie couldn't help but bait him. He'd been so stoic and "correct," taunting him had become a great source of amusement.

Ben shook his head. "Shut up, smartass. C'mon. We might as well go over and introduce ourselves."

Marie looked at the tall, willowy blonde and rolled her eyes. "Sure, let's go make nice with the woman who almost killed me."

"She must have been scared of everything going on around her. Demons possessing people, black shadows floating in the air looking for another host, people killing people. It's not exactly what your average human expects to see every day, never mind most of them have no training or preparation for what's coming." Ben's defense of the pretty woman hurt Marie, which pissed her off even more. She hated that she compared herself to *Raine*, and hated more that she cared about Ben's assessment of the differences between the two women.

"Sure," Marie said without looking at Ben. "Let's go say hello." *So I can break both her arms.*

Marie could feel Ben's scrutiny, but she refused to acknowledge him. She stood and began walking in the young woman's direction. Ben caught up, and they walked across the courtyard and to greet the new arrival.

Raine's brown eyes rounded when she caught sight of the two of them headed her way. Ben raised his hand and waved at her before the woman had a chance to disappear back inside her room.

"Hello. I'm Texas State Trooper, Ben Brown." His voice was calm and reassuring.

Niiice. He'd had never talked to Marie in that tone. Hell, for weeks he'd barely talked to her at all. Why he'd decided to be buddy-buddy, she had no idea, but she was beginning to miss his silence. At least then she could insert whatever thoughts or conversation she wanted into his head and mouth.

Watching him be all nonthreatening made her bristle, at the same time she had to give him credit. Clearly he'd used his title in an attempt to assuage the woman's worries. Good thing the new arrival didn't have a gun this time around because, the way the woman was looking at her, Marie would have already been full of holes.

"You're a cop?" Raine asked while taking a tentative step forward. "A real cop. A human cop?"

"Well, I'd say that I'm roughly fifty-percent human, give or take. The same as you are." Ben made his tone soft and welcoming. Why hadn't she gotten this version of Ben? With her, he was sarcastic, bossy, and argumentative, the rare times he did more than scowl at her..

"No, I'm not an animal like her," Raine said while pointing an accusing, perfectly manicured finger straight at Marie. "They're trying to convince me that I'm one of them, but I know better." She made a gagging noise and shuddered. "Disgusting."

Marie couldn't help but growl. She'd never liked it when someone pointed at her. Since her failed attempt to overthrow the matriarch of the clan, that gesture had been happening more frequently. The taunts had been utterly merciless, and made her feel like she was back in her cell.

"Because of animals like me," Marie snarled, "your ass is still alive, princess. Show some respect."

"You people kidnapped me," Raine spat out.

"We saved you," Marie corrected. "Would you have preferred to stay where you were waiting for death to come for you? 'Cause I'd be more than happy to arrange that *tout suite*."

Why was she even bothering? This hybrid hated everything about her shifter side without even knowing what being a shifter meant and what she was missing. And talk about ungrateful. Marie wasn't going to waste her time when there were so many more important things to do.

Before she had a chance to walk away, the sound of footsteps coming toward them from down the hall interrupted the *riveting* conversation. Marie would have been grateful for the interruption if it weren't the three male wolf-shifters who came walking around the corner. She recognized all of them from the rescue party she'd been on days earlier. One was the guy who questioned how anyone could ever trust her again.

"Great, this is all I need," Marie grumbled as she walked over to cut the three off before they could get too far into the human-shifters' courtyard. "What are you three doing here? You know this area's off-limits."

The same wolf continued to look behind Marie at what she assumed had to be Ben and Raine, but she knew better than to turn her back on the wolves.

"We've come to talk to you," he said before gesturing toward the men beside him. "I'm Joseph, from the North Woods pack, and this is Thomas and Rellon."

"I've already heard what you have to say before we left on the last mission. As I remember it, you questioned my loyalty to the clan. Wondering how anyone could ever trust me." The same sentiment had been repeated regularly in many different ways.

She heard the growl from behind her before she even finished the sentence. Ben. What was that all about?

Nothing could have prepared Marie for Joseph's expression. Shame and regret. "Yes, I did, and that's why we came."

Her sharp black claws lengthened by several inches. "You came to discuss my loyalty."

The gasp coming from behind her was the final straw, and Marie finally glanced back to find Raine pressed up against Ben's side with her hands wrapped around his tattooed bicep and nails digging into his flesh.

Yep, that's about right. Trooper, protect her from the beast. It never got old.

"No, I came to apologize," Joseph said. "We're sorry for doubting you. After watching you throw yourself in front of a bullet for Goddess Zahra, a wolf-shifter, we knew we had been wrong. That shot would have killed you, yet you didn't hesitate."

When she'd walked over to the wolves, of all possible ways she'd had thought this conversation was going to go, Joseph's statements weren't close to what Marie had expected. Given her experience to date, she wasn't quite sure how to respond.

Before she could form her response, she noticed that Joseph was having a hard time keeping his eyes off Raine. Who could blame him? She was beautiful and delicate with her thin frame, and she exuded vulnerability, which for some stupid reason made men fall all over themselves to care for her. *We're shifters. We're supposed to be able to take care of ourselves and our packs. What the hell is wrong with men?* Ugh.

"You jumped in front of another bullet?" Ben snapped, and she realized she hadn't shared that bit of information with him yet. "One hole in your body wasn't enough?"

"Not now." Marie had had enough for one day. She nodded at the wolves. "I accept your apologies. Now, if you could find your way back out. I've been ordered to rest by the clan doctor."

Yeah, yeah, she'd been ignoring those instructions all day, but right now they came in handy.

Peace and quiet, that's what she yearned for. In the absence of a regular life, closing her eyes and imaging the world as it used to be was her only solace. Picturing herself aboveground, she'd have let her bear out for a run. In her mind, she could almost feel the sun's rays warming her fur as she stretched her muscles and inhaled the forest's musty aroma.

"Of course," Joseph agreed. "Also, in the interest of learning more about the human-shifters, may I come back to speak with them?"

Marie knew who it was he wanted to get to know better, but that wasn't her call. "That's up to the alpha triads. If they say it's okay, then I have no problem with it."

"Understood. Thank you for your time, and again, I apologize for ever doubting you." He bowed his head slightly, then the three wolf-shifters turned to leave, but not before Joseph took one last look at Raine. Gods help her with having to deal with all the testosterone floating around the room.

Marie considered returning to the conversation with Ben and Raine, then decided against it. She didn't bother looking back. Best to leave the two human-shifters alone. If anyone could bring Miss Priss around and get her to acknowledge the realities of life, never mind her shifter side, Ben could.

"I'm going to rest," Marie announced. When she heard Ben take a breath in as if preparing to speak, she continued, "I don't wish to be disturbed. I'm sure you can handle everything out here, Trooper."

Without waiting for a reply, she walked away. She wished the sight of Ben holding the newcomer in his arms wouldn't bite as much as it did. That she'd never be dainty was a fact, that she'd never be helpless again was a promise she'd made to herself. Let the poor defenseless hybrid cling. She'd learn that if she didn't take care of herself, she'd become a casualty of war. No dying swans and frippy faeries were going to make it out of this shit alive.

Right before she locked the solid door to her private domain, she heard Raine's tinkling laughter echoing through the courtyard. Marie closed her eyes and took a deep breath.

Her private area wasn't much. Marie didn't have a lot. She glanced over at her bedroom dresser to assure herself the small box was still beside the table lamp where she'd left it.

Rose had recovered the contents Marie had hidden behind a wall inside the cell that her parents had kept her locked in. That small collection was the only real *things* she'd ever owned. The matriarch had given Marie everything else in her possession to navigate through everyday life.

It wasn't lost on her that after so many years of living, all Marie had to show for it was the contents of a two by four inch box.

Chapter Five

Ben did everything in his power to extricate his arm from Raine's hold, short of physically pushing her away.

"That was so scary. Did you see its claws come shooting out?" she gasped. "Animals, vicious animals, every last one of them. They probably brought me here to be used as some freaky sacrifice."

After hearing what the rude, insensitive, ungrateful woman had to say, Ben ripped his arm free of her grasp, but the cloying diva made sure she left a few scratch marks on his skin. He was sure she thought it was a sexy gift he'd look at and think of her and her *helplessness*.

"Let me say this once more, because it's apparent that the first couple of times you weren't listening too closely. You're partially a shifter, like me. I'm grizzly, and you, well, I have no idea what animal you share your lifeforce with. Didn't your parents ever explain to you why you were different?"

Raine reared back as if he'd slapped her. "I'm not a freak. I was homecoming queen. My life was perfect. I was studying fashion and had finally been offered a coveted internship in Paris. I was going to learn from the greats, then you people, and whatever is out there, came and destroyed it." She stomped her right foot for good measure before storming off and locking herself back inside the room she'd been assigned.

Ben looked between the two closed doors, one Marie's, the other Raine's, on either side of the common area, unsure of what the hell had happened.

Raine, he understood. Her perfect life, as she called it, was gone, and she was being told that shifters and demons were real, among many other species thought to be myth and fantasy. To top it off, telling her that she is one of them toppled her carefully constructed world. Her plans had not included Collector Demons and discovering she was a shifter hybrid.

Little did she know, she was vicious just the same. The one time the hunters had come through his territory, he'd heard those terms before: beast, animal, and the like. The words made his skin crawl and the grizzly inside him wanted to swipe at them with a massive paw.

He understood why Marie had stormed off. She'd suffered enough abuse for several human lifetimes. What he couldn't wrap his mind around was why she hadn't told him about the second bullet that could have killed her. Knowing he wasn't going to get any answers standing alone in the courtyard, he headed toward what was his second mission of the day.

An excellent sense of direction was essential in this maze of halls beneath the earth, and he was grateful he had a bear's senses, or he would have been lost a couple times over by the time he reached the alpha triad's office. Two massive bear-shifters stood on either side of the closed double doors. Neither bothered to look at him.

"I've come to speak with the alpha triad," he said. Ben hoped there wasn't an official channel or some hoops he needed to jump through first.

While the one farthest away growled, the other said, "They cannot be disturbed."

"Okay." That was utterly understandable with everything that's happened. "Do you know of a better time for me to come back?"

"Nev—" the warrior began to say before he was interrupted.

"Edmund, is there a problem?" Mason, the bear clan alpha asked from the now-open office doors.

"No, Alpha. I was advising the human-shifter—"

"Ben." Mason's voice was cold as ice and the guard swallowed hard.

"Yes, Alpha. I was advising Ben that you do not wish to be disturbed."

Ben watched the exchange with fascination. The entire time he wondered how powerful Mason had to be to make even the largest of bears quake.

"Well, isn't it fortunate indeed that we are now available for fellow clan members?"

"Yes, Alpha," Edmund replied.

"We will discuss this later," Mason warned, and both warriors lowered their heads.

Mason turned his attention onto Ben. "How may we help you?" he asked while walking back into his office. Ben followed.

"I need to go to the surface."

"The surface?" Riker asked from his perch on the couch beside Matriarch Rose. Why would you want to risk doing that?"

"It's not safe for you to return aboveground. The Collector Demons may not be able to infect you, but they surely can kill you," Rose explained.

"I realize it's a lot to ask, but my mother is out there, and I have to go get her. She's full shifter, so she wouldn't have been infected and has to be hiding."

"How would you know where to even find her?" Mason asked.

"We have this place in the mountains outside my hometown. If anything ever happened, we swore to meet there."

"And that's where you want to go?" Rose asked.

"Yes. I need to check if my mom's waiting there for me to return," Ben replied. "I can't leave her out there. Please."

Ben didn't appreciate being beholden to anyone, but if they agreed, he'd repay their kindness in spades.

"I can teleport us," Rose offered. "I'd have to access your memories to get an exact location, though."

"Access anything you need," Ben stated.

"Mate, if you think you're going to traipse around a mountain without one of us, you're wrong," Mason clarified.

"And a group of our best warriors," Riker added.

"And me," Marie's tired voice rang out from behind him.

Ben spun around to face her. "You're supposed to be resting and recovering from a gunshot wound for Christ's sakes."

Marie's eyes got that same glint in them when something pissed her off. She was looking down at his arm, or, more specifically, the scratches left by Raine. Why did he suddenly feel guilty?

"This has nothing to do with you, Trooper. I will protect my matriarch."

"It's decided then," Rose's voice cut through the tension, which made Ben face the triad again. "We'll head out at first light tomorrow. We can all meet in the boardroom."

Ben was elated and worried at the same time. "Thank you, Alpha Triad."

When he turned around for the second time to leave, Marie was nowhere in sight. She'd been upset, and that tore at his gut. Yes, he wanted her to be happy, to have the shit that had been heaped on her a distant memory, but he'd never thought of her as anything more than part of the group that saved them. Then, one day, he caught her scent in the gym, and like a thunderbolt, she became the only thing he seemed to be able to focus on. Then, when she was hurt, he thought he'd jump out of his skin with worry. He'd heard about instant attraction before, but this was several light years beyond that.

What's wrong with me?

***

Marie's lean muscles flexed and stretched with every move. The substantial weight in her hands felt comforting and reassuring. She wrapped her hands around the cold steel and gripped the metal bar tightly before bench-pressing five-hundred pounds of circular steel as if it weighed a paltry fifty pounds.

Shifters didn't need to work out to stay in shape. Their species determined their general strength, and within each pack there were warriors and there were civilians. But no one was weak. Bear were among the strongest shifters, while smaller animals relied on cunning and speed to keep themselves alive.

Generally, working out wasn't part of her routine. But she was stuck underground and she needed to burn off steam. She was angry with herself for reacting to Ben so strongly. He infuriated her in a way no one had before. And when she saw that simpering hybrid's nail marks on his arm, Marie nearly lost it. In an attempt not to embarrass herself further, she figured working out would help. To the uninitiated, seeing a five-foot-nine inch woman lifting hundreds of pounds might have seemed impossible. But when she was in her bear form, she was over seven feet tall and weighed about six hundred pounds. To say her strength was deceptive in human form was an understatement.

As for Ben, she'd do well to remember he was a hybrid, and as such he was her responsibility, nothing more. She had to get herself back under control.

"Planning a long workout as opposed to resting?" Rose asked as she sat down on the bench beside her.

Marie didn't miss a beat in her reps. "Staying in my room was driving me crazy."

"What's got you so twisted up?" Rose asked.

There was no way Marie was sharing her thoughts and feelings with Rose. She'd think Marie had gone over the edge. Ben was a hybrid who needed her protection, not her insane jealousy.

"My bear is restless, that's all."

"Hmm, I can understand that," Rose said. "How about we spar for a bit? I could use a stress reliever myself."

Without waiting for an answer, her friend stood and walked into the gymnasium that was adjacent to the weight room. Marie set the barbells back into their cradles and, with a loud huff, got up to join her matriarch.

Sparring between shifters was quite a bit different than human boxing or wrestling. An inevitable truth: blood would be spilled. Their strength, power, and agility guaranteed a no-holding back approach, even though they were only blowing off steam. There weren't any official rules, only agreements between opponents, such as not inflicting injuries severe enough to warrant the infirmary. A few claw marks and bruises would heal quickly enough.

Marie stepped behind one of several canvas privacy screens lined up around the perimeter of the massive room. Considering their combined pack and clan couldn't go outside, they had to make do with this area when times like this arose.

The alpha triads had made sure to have screens installed in various locations since Jenny, Matthew, and Ben had arrived. To shifters, nudity was a regular occurrence, but those raised in the human world weren't as comfortable seeing people walking around without clothing.

Piece by piece, she removed her clothing in preparation to shift into her bear. Her excitement at what was to come bubbled over. The transformation was effortless, her bear was eager to get out and stretch. She vocalized a few deep huffs and a low growl in happiness. Marie flexed each of her four paws, allowing her sharp claws to extend.

It felt good to be back in her animal form. Every muscle and sense humming in readiness for the battle to begin.

She ambled around the screen and onto the thick mats covering the sparring area. Her sharp nails dug into the material, but they never puncture through. Raz had used her goddess mojo-powers on them so that they wouldn't tear and have to be replaced. It wasn't as if they could send out for more.

Marie sat down on the padding to wait for her matriarch to join her. She wasn't surprised by the sight of the stunning white wolf almost the size of a full-grown bear walking from behind the screen at the opposite end of the gym. Rose was no ordinary wolf. She was the reincarnation of the Goddess Thorne and had the powers to back it up.

While she was thinking about it, Marie asked through their personal link, *"No using powers, right?"*

"No powers. That wouldn't be fair," Rose agreed.

"You're going to kick my ass anyway, but a workout sounds perfect."

Rose took her spot as Maria did the same.

"Shall we say whoever reaches three pins is the winner," Rose suggested.

"That seems long enough to get my head on straight."

"Game on."

Marie dug her claws in deep ready to charge forward. Rose, of course, looked as if she were merely going for a run, which was fitting. As alpha matriarch, Rose was physically stronger than anyone else in the clan, except for her mates whom she equaled, even without her goddess abilities. The only way to be able to get in a few shots with such a powerful opponent was skill and patience.

They stalked toward the center, sizing each other up as they neared. Marie used all her senses to try to predict when Rose would make her move. Marie had seen Rose fight. The matriarch was unpredictable, making her all the more dangerous.

Marie didn't have to wait long. One of the muscles in Rose's front right leg flexed and gave her away. The wolf raced straight toward her, but Marie used her half second advantage to shift her substantial body enough so her friend's claws narrowly missed her side, while Marie inflicted her own strike to one of Rose's hind legs.

They turned to face each other once again. The scent of blood filled the room even though Marie had pulled back from delivering a more profound blow.

"Nice work," Rose said with pride. *"Have you been practicing?"*

To the outside world, it might be odd for the bleeding person to complement the one who'd inflicted the blow. Again, different worlds. This was practice, not a real fight.

"I've grown accustomed to predicting others' first moves," Marie said without going into a deep explanation. Rose knew the hell Marie's life had been.

Rose nodded her head. *"I see. Has that particular skill come in handy here in the bunkers?"*

Marie knew what she was asking: had others taken shots at her since the truth about her family came out. Matriarch Rose's strength was surpassed only by her heart.

"Everything is fine for me here." There was no way she'd add to her friend's list of worries. Marie knew Rose wouldn't buy it, but thankfully she let it go.

The two began circling each other once again. *"So, are you going to tell me what's really got you angry?"*

"You mean other than being stuck underground because Collector Demons roam the earth?"

"Are you sure? I would have thought the scratches on Ben's arm would have set you off."

How did she know? Was something said? Had she been too obvious? How many other people knew?

Instead of answering, Marie's bear charged at her opponent in an attempt to squash any further talk about Ben. Of course, it was a bone-headed, emotionally driven move, and she deserved the pain she was about to receive from Rose's claws.

Sure enough, the first blow scraped along her side, and she found herself flying through the air, landing on her back several feet away. Before she could get up, Rose jumped on top of her, effectively pinning Marie to the ground.

"I'll take your response to mean that I've hit the mark. This is about Ben."

"Leave it alone."

"How can I when I see my friend in a downward spiral," Rose argued before lifting off her. *"You're risking your life every chance you get, and now your mind is consumed by a human-shifter you'd be better off avoiding."*

"What does it matter? I've gotten to choose what I do with my life since the moment my parents were killed. I've had enough of

other people determining my future." Marie got to her feet and surveyed the damage to her side. It wasn't as bad as it could have been.

"I understand that and I'm not trying to tell you what to do. I'm concerned the next bullet will be your last."

"If it's my time, then nothing's going to stop it."

"And that's that, is it?"

"Yeah, it is."

Rose charged at her again, but this time Marie was able to spin out of the way. She turned around in time to see her friend use the steel wall as a springboard to change direction, however, not fast enough for her to get out of the way this time.

With a bone-rattling crash, Marie was sent to the ground for a second time, but before she could be pinned, she lifted her hind legs and catapulted the matriarch across the room.

"What is wrong with you?" Marie asked as she got back to her feet.

"What's wrong with me?" Rose growled as she continued to stalk forward. *"I'm not the one who'd sooner die and leave those human children, her friends, and her mate behind to grieve the loss."*

Rose attacked head-on. They both rose to their hind legs and began trading blows with their paws. Thanks to Marie's thick fur, many of the hits never made it through to her skin. Rose held back to make the battle almost even. As Marie gasped for breath, Rose's words finally began penetrating the fog of anger.

"Mate?"

She didn't even see the claws coming before Marie found herself flat on her back once again. This time there was no getting up as Rose landed on top of her and took hold of her throat.

"I give. Now, what the hell do you mean by mate?" Marie growled as she pushed Rose off to the side.

"I didn't intend to say that, but you get me so pissed when you're cavalier about your own life."

"And?" Marie wasn't letting this go.

"Ben, for heaven's sakes. Ben."

Marie wasn't sure if she was still breathing. Everything had gone quiet. Her human mind went blank as her bear began to work out what she had been told. Ben's scent was more than intoxicating, it drew her like he was made for her. Her jealousy over Raine, who was such a silly thing. Had anyone else paid the hybrid any attention, Marie would've razzed them for day. Then there was the need to be around him. Like always. At first she'd thought the attraction was because he was something, someone so new and different to their culture, he was a rarity worthy of examination. She had to admit, watching over him was no hardship. The man was a delicious specimen. When her curiosity had morphed into something more, she couldn't say, but now, she had to admit, the likelihood the human-shifter was her mate seemed...true?

This made less sense than usual. He wasn't fully a bear. Did he even have the capcity to mate? Then there was the fact that Marie was nobody. The least deserving of them all.

Marie had no recollection of what motivated her, but she stood and headed for the door, still in her bear form. She was wandering down the corridors and realized she was heading toward her room. People flattened themselves against the walls or ducked into open doorways. Vaguely, she noted these halls were made for human form, and that she had to be a sight in bear form, especially covered in wounds and blood.

When she entered the restricted area, Ben came running toward her from across the courtyard."What happened to you? Who did this?" he shouted.

Instead of answering, her bear only had one thing on its mind. She stuck her muzzle against Ben's chest and took in a deep breath. *Damn.* His scent belonged to her. Somehow, this craziness made sense. How had she missed this? And why her?

With a small huff, Marie retreated into her room and shoved the door shut with her massive head.

This was wrong on every level. She didn't deserve a mate. He was a hybrid. There was a war going on. She had nothing to offer him. And, most importantly, if he were to mate with her—the most vilified person belowground, no matter how the alpha triad treated her—she would destroy Ben's chances of ever being accepted by the clan.

When would the gods be done punishing her?

Chapter Six

After locking herself in her room, Marie had shifted back into human form, lay on her side on top of her bedcovers, and stared at the wall while she'd turned over the whole Ben is her mate problem. Several hours passed until the only viable solution presented itself. If nobody suspected the truth, then the clan couldn't hold the fact that they were fated mates against Ben. Odd how months ago she'd have been more concerned about how being fated mates with a human-shifter affected her own precarious standing. Time and circumstances changed everyone's perspective.

She'd gotten to know the man by that time, and Marie had to admit that she liked him. What you saw was what you got when it came to him. Loathsome, cruel, self-serving people had surrounded her since birth, and she found it refreshing and comforting to know someone who wasn't continuously plotting, scheming, or hiding his true self. That she'd been physically attracted to him from the first moment she laid her eyes on him was another matter entirely.

Marie could never act on those impulses.

While a few shifters had thawed toward her, it wasn't nearly enough to consider dragging Ben into her special kind of screwed up life. Everyone would be more apt to accept him if he wasn't involved with her in any way.

Now, she was sitting in a conference room, having been summoned to a meeting.

"So, want to tell me why you're all the way over here on the opposite side of the boardroom from Ben?" Rose asked as she sat down beside Marie.

"It's better to keep my distance," she responded. "No one needs to know the truth."

"I never took you to be a human hater," Rose said sharply.

"This isn't about him, it's about me. He can't be saddled with someone like me if he ever wants a life among the clan."

Marie looked away from her friend to find Ben staring at her. He wore his police-issued bulletproof vest over a dark, long-sleeved shirt that stretched around his sizeable biceps. His eyes seemed impossibly more mysterious, to the point of being almost forest green, and the set of his jaw spoke to how angry he was.

Of course, anything could've riled him up, but Marie avoiding him since returning to her room the night before might be to blame. If he knew the truth, she was sure he'd understand her reasoning, and even support it.

"You are not a virus, Marie," Rose argued. "You're not contagious."

"Wanna bet?" she countered. "Do you see anyone clamoring to be near me, or asking me to join in anything at all? Trust me, being in the restricted area isn't the only reason I don't have visitors. We both know this, Matriarch. You need to accept the truth."

"I heard Joseph came by to apologize for his rather brutal comment," Rose said. "It's a start."

"Yeah, and all that took was for me to stand in front of a bullet while bleeding out from a different bullet. Hate to see what it takes for the remaining hundreds to come around."

"But—"

"There are no buts. What I need is for you to be my friend and understand it's for the best. Once we get his mother back here, it will be easier for others to accept Ben since she's a full shifter. Since there'll be another bear to protect him and the children, I'm moving after his mother has acclimated herself."

Rose stared at her for a long moment, but nothing, not even her matriarch's opinions would change Marie's mind. She knew keeping her distance from Ben would be the only way to ensure a smooth transition for him and his mother.

"This discussion isn't over," Rose said before standing and joining her mates at the front of the room.

Marie couldn't help but smile at her friend's tenacity, but there would be no further discussions. She was the only one who knew plans were already in the works for her to move to the far end of the facility, and nothing would change that. How did the old adage go? Out of sight, out of mind.

"Okay, everyone, now that the team is complete, I'd like your attention on the screen," John announced, causing the room to quiet and for everyone to turn to the front overhead television screen. "This is a map of the area we'll be searching today. As you can see, the terrain is rugged in spots, and we'll only be a quarter mile out of the nearest town, increasing the chances we might run into Collectors in the area."

Ben stood and walked to the front to join the alpha triads. "As you all know, this is a mission to find and bring back my mother. Her name is Joan, and she is a bear-shifter, so there's a chance she's still alive." His voice wavered slightly squeezing Marie's heart. "This is a voluntary group. If you don't want to risk yourself, no harm, no foul, you can remain here. To those who come along, thank you for giving me a chance to find her."

Marie looked around the room at the combined shifter force assembled and noted a few nods and whispered agreements to help, giving her all the more reason to keep her distance. Clearly, a few people had begun viewing Ben differently.

After they received their final instructions, their team joined hands, and Rose transported them all to the location in north Texas she'd had taken from Ben's memories. Wisely, their matriarch brought them down in the thick of an old forest filled with oak and elm trees. No one wanted to be caught out in the open. Rose had impressive goddess powers, but even she had her limits protecting everyone if they were overrun by demons.

Raz and Zahra hadn't joined them on this journey. They couldn't risk having all three goddesses away from the protection of the bunker at the same time until they could get better control over the movements of the demons on the surface.

The group spread out around the clan's alpha triad. Marie had been given the position as a scout and headed north ahead of their party to keep an eye out for any signs of Ben's mother and the Collectors. With her sword strapped at a slant across her back, explosives clipped to her belt, and a high-powered rifle in her hands, Marie raced ahead.

She kept to the shadows and behind cover as much as possible. In the distance, she could make out the silhouette of a small town, and wondered if that was where Ben had grown up. As if the mere thought of him conjured the man out of thin air, he came up the trail behind her.

"Don't recall there being two scouts on this mission," Marie whispered by way of welcome.

"Thought you could use some help considering I grew up in these woods."

"I'm good at what I do. There's no fear of me leading us into trouble." Marie moved swiftly to the next stand of trees. "I'll be fine on my own."

"Yeah, I've seen how good you are at it," Ben shot back as he crouched down beside her. "What's your problem anyway?"

"You want to discuss this right now?" Marie asked in a harsh whisper while turning to look back at him. Ben was only a few inches away. Had he always had brown flecks in his eyes? Their lips were almost close enough to touch.

She zeroed in on those lips and couldn't help but wonder if they were as soft as they looked. She felt the pull, and as if he knew her thoughts and what her body yearned for, he had the nerve to grin in his sexy-ass way. She felt the urge to strangle him.

She turned away and began forward again, taking tight control over herself and concentrating on their surroundings. The odd hawk cried out as it went about hunting while rabbits and mice ran for their burrows to avoid becoming dinner. The sound of rushing water alerted her that they were getting closer to the cave where, with any luck, Joan would be waiting.

After about ten more minutes, they came to a ridge overlooking the stream, and a short walk beyond, she could make out the opening to a cave.

"Is this it?" she asked Ben, once he'd crawled up to take the position beside her.

"Yeah."

She relayed the information back to their team through the link. Ben scented the air in much the same way as Marie was doing.

"We're too far away to get a solid scent," she said. "We'll wait for the team before going to check it out."

"Maybe it's best if I approach alone. She could be scared or wounded," he said, and Marie could feel the pain behind those words.

"I understand your thinking, but I can't risk you running into a Collector Demon," she stated. "The rest of the team is only minutes away. If I see anything indicating a danger to your mother, I swear I'll be the first one down the hill."

Ben didn't agree, but he didn't go off to the cave on his own. She figured her logic and strategy had somehow penetrated. As she'd predicted, Rose, her mates, and the rest arrived and began discussing options on the best way to approach the cave.

"I'll go down there with Ben and six warriors," Mason stated. "Rose, Riker, Marie, and the four remaining warriors will remain here to cover us in case of attack."

"In case of attack, right. You don't want me down there," Rose responded with a shake of her head.

"There's that as well." Mason nodded. "Let's go."

Marie turned to find Ben looking at her, and no matter how hard she fought the words, she couldn't help but say, "Be safe."

With his brilliant smile back in place, Ben winked at her, and he left with the others.

"You're doing a great job at this distancing thing," Rose whispered, not even trying to hide her chuckle.

"Shut up," Marie growled softly at her smiling friend.

They both turned their heads to keep an eye on their team descending into the gulley. With every move they made, Marie calculated the time it would take her to get down there if this was somehow a trap. Who knew if the Collectors had already found Joan and were waiting around for more shifters to arrive. Though she would prefer not to think of Ben's mother in the demons' hands.

Her team spread out over the ridge, taking offensive positions in case anything went wrong at the last moment. The area was quiet. Nothing seemed out of place, which made Marie even edgier. It felt as if the world was holding its breath as the team in the gulley surrounded the dark opening.

When Ben took several steps closer to the mouth of the cave, Marie growled. *"Don't you even think about going in there alone."*

When Ben answered, she was reminded that the alpha triads had gifted him with the ability to access the link after she'd been shot. *"See. I knew you cared."*

"Don't be a fool. I simply don't want all my hard work keeping you alive this long to go to waste." Even though Marie couldn't see his facial features, she was positive the sexy jerk was grinning. *"Don't let it go to your head."*

"Don't worry, growly, you keep my feet on the ground like no other."

Marie wasn't one-hundred-percent sure if that was a compliment, but she didn't have time to mull it over as Ben, Mason, and two warriors vanished inside of the cave.

It felt like pins were prickling all over her skin once she lost sight of him. So far, this whole mate situation wasn't endearing itself to her. If she wasn't angry, she was panicked. These emotions were far too similar to the ones she'd felt living inside a cell.

Seconds ticked by, and still no movement. Marie was nearing her last shred of patience when the alpha and Ben emerged from the darkness. However, his mother was nowhere in sight.

Before she had a chance to question him, a lone red-tailed hawk glided above them. Marie was unsure if it was the same hawk she'd heard earlier, but there was one thing she was positive about, that hawk was a shifter.

Slowly, it circled lower until it came to land on a rocky outcropping several feet away. Marie instinctively moved closer to Rose, unsure of the shifter's friendliness. She glanced down to confirm Ben and the others were on their way back up the ridge before centering her complete attention on the bird.

"We're not here to harm you," Rose began. "We've come hoping to find our friend's mother. She's a bear-shifter."

The hawk hopped down onto a flatter surface, never taking its eyes off them. The other half of their team climbed up over the ridge and quietly joined them.

The bird looked to be trying to make a decision.

Ben stepped forward. "Please, I'm looking for my mother, have you seen anyone near here?"

The raw emotion in his voice drove Marie to try to comfort him, and, uncharacteristically, she placed her hand on his shoulder and squeezed. That was the best she could do, but it appeared to be enough as his stiff shoulders relaxed the tiniest bit.

The red-tailed hawk gave out one last cry before initiating the shift and revealing a young boy, maybe seven or eight years old. Ben pulled a small pack from one of the pockets on his vest and unrolled it into a windbreaker jacket. He took a few more steps and held it out to the boy, who accepted it and pulled it over his head. The trooper's jacket went well past the child's knees.

"Thank you," the boy said.

"Sweetie, are you out here all alone?" Rose asked.

Had the poor little guy been abandoned, or was his family victims of the new world order? Either way, Marie knew they could take care of him back at the bunker. The boy would never have to worry about anything, and maybe Jenny and Matthew would gain a playmate.

"A-huh. They took my parents and the rest of my flock," he explained with a rough voice.

Marie grabbed her canteen from her side and opened it before handing it over to the child. "What's your name?"

"Tim. Timothy."

"Okay, Tim," Mason said. "You're safe now. We have a place where you won't have to worry about the Collectors any more."

Tim's eyes brightened. "You have more people?"

"A lot more people."

The boy downed a few good gulps of water before saying, "Then, you can save them."

"Them?"

"My parents and the flock."

"You know where they are?"

"Yes," he said before pointing at Ben. "They're with his mom."

Chapter Seven

Ben wasn't sure what he was looking at, but he knew it was all kinds of wrong. Cages lined the walls as far as he could see in all directions. Their team made sure to stay far enough away as to not arouse anyone's attention. Shifter eyesight, enhanced further by high-powered binoculars, assured they remained concealed.

Rose had used Tim's memories to locate the facility and to bring them there. The Collectors looked to have set up shop in an abandoned roadside zoo, replacing the typical animals with shifters. Cages held several different species from across North America and beyond. The question was, how were they able to get them here.

As far as Ben knew, once a Collector took possession of a human body, most of the host's advanced human-based skills were lost, such as driving, flying, among others. Too bad the same thing couldn't be said for all the ways the Collectors were able to wreak havoc and destruction.

"What the hell is this?" John asked, his voice shaking with anger. "They're stockpiling shifters."

"I never understood zoos to begin with. Humans should have protected these animals in the wild before decimating their numbers and causing mass extinctions, taking what's left to be gawked at and used to repopulate their numbers while still allowing hunters to kill them in the wild." Ben shook his head. "This shit right here adds a new layer of disgust." Ben growled, making a few warriors look his way.

The thought of his mother in there somewhere enraged him. If he ever could have gone furry, now would have been one of those times.

Tactically, the team had one advantage. The zoo was located on the outskirts of a small city a couple hundred miles away from the cave. There weren't many buildings around it to block their view. On the other hand, buildings provided cover, and, although the

Collector Demons weren't expecting to be raided, the team would be out in the open and easy to pick off.

"Gather all the intelligence you can on this place," Mason ordered. "Numbers of shifters and Collectors, escape routes, old maps of the zoo if we can find any online, and the demons patrol routines. We'll head back to the bunkers and come up with a plan of attack. This is going to take a whole lot more muscle and power then we have here at the moment."

Ben understood the reasoning, but it didn't make it any easier to leave his mom in that place one moment longer. What was even worse was the possibility that she wasn't in a cage down there any longer, that she'd been moved, or worse.

He felt her presence long before Marie crawled over to his lookout position. That feeling had been happening more often recently anytime she was near him. Such an odd thing to feel his entire body reach out to hers, and to only feel calm when she was by his side. Yesterday's whole vanishing act had driven him crazy, and to find her covered in bloody injuries when she'd returned had him shaking with fear and anger. Typically, he had his emotions under control, locked down tight. He wouldn't have been effective as a Trooper otherwise. But now? She made his heart skips beats, or thunder in his chest. He was tied to her physically, mentally, and emotionally.

At least Hope took mercy on him, and explained that Marie and Rose had been sparring, which explained the blood. However, he still didn't have an answer to her repeated disappearances and increased physical distances when they were in the same area.

"We'll get your mother out of there. I promise," she said.

Ben soaked in the peace she brought him, which only intensified when she touched him. Her dark eyes held so many emotions that he wished she would share with him. But, aside from her acting the good battle colleague, she made herself scarce.

"You can't promise that. We don't know what we're up against, or if my mother's even there." Ben fought to keep despair from his voice. "But, if there's a chance for us to save those other shifters, she'd be proud of us if we accomplished that."

"She sounds like an amazing woman. Raising you as a single mother without the help of a clan."

"Oh, that wasn't by her choice," Ben explained. "She was thrown out of her birth clan when she admitted to being pregnant with me."

"Seriously? That's bullshit," Marie grumbled, pleasing him that she was angry on his and his mom's behalf.

"My father was human, that was enough for the clan to exile us," he said. "My mother is bear-shifter, and that was enough for my father to desert us." So many people had made decisions about him and his life before Ben had even been born.

"Our people had no idea human-shifters even existed until the Sun God Ra chose Zahra to find as many as she could and protect them."

"Funny, one god wants to save us, while our own people are embarrassed about our existence. Sad how real life plays out some times."

Rose came over to join them. "Ready to go?" They both nodded. "Good, we have work to do. Let's go."

The three of them crawled back behind a wall of rock before standing alongside the rest of their team with their newest member, Timothy. They joined hands, and as before, when Ben opened his eyelids, they were back in the boardroom deep within the earth.

Safe, but without his mother. Ben swore that if she was somewhere inside that roadside zoo, he wouldn't be returning without her the next time.

***

Marie knew what she was doing was all kinds of stupid, but the driving need to make sure Ben was all right had forced her to this point. He'd left the meeting hours ago and hadn't returned. She couldn't hope to understand what he was going through, considering the lack of a relationship she'd had with her mother, a mother who caged her child, and inflicted all type of torture upon her. Even though Marie couldn't empathize, she could be his sounding board if he needed to talk.

Following his scent was easy. Hell, her entire body was honed in on it by now. Given the hour, it was no surprise when she found the courtyard in their private area dark. She had brought Tim to stay with Hope and the other children when they'd first arrived back at their base. Marie wished his parents were still alive, but didn't have a good feeling about it. Knowing he'd be well cared for was a comfort, but it'd take him a long time to get past the grief of losing his family.

The low hum of anger pulsing through her body throttled up at the thought of all of the orphans and the dead who had fallen at the hands of the demons.

When she reached his room, Ben's door was ajar, and she could hear a guitar softly playing. She didn't know if it was him or a recording. When she knocked on the door, there was no response, but the chords played on. Slowly she pushed the door all the way open until she could get a better look inside. The rooms were dark except for a single lamp glowing softly in the far corner of the living room beside the couch.

A lone figure sat with his broad back to her, strumming what sounded like a familiar song. Where had he found a guitar? Then the song's name came to her, "What a Wonderful World" made famous by Louis Armstrong. The chords seemed sad and vibrated deep inside her as the words floated through her head.

"I see skies of blue…"

"And clouds of white…" Ben replied through the link, but he still hadn't turned around to look at her.

"Can I get you anything?" *That's the best I can come up with?* Marie didn't think he'd appreciate being asked if he was okay. Clearly, she hadn't thought this through.

"No. I'm fine. Thanks for the offer." His voice was cold and lifeless.

She was so unpracticed at social nicities she felt beyone awkward. Certain his mind was back at the zoo, she didn't know how to comfort him, but she figured if he had company he might feel better. "Do you mind if I join you?"

He shrugged his shoulders. "Sit if you want."

She'd had worse offers, and that he hadn't sent her away was a good sign. "Okay, for a bit." Marie walked around the back of the couch and sat on the end opposite Ben. "Who taught you to play the guitar?"

The words were out before she'd actually thought it through. If his mom had taught him, Marie would feel horrible for bringing it up. On the other hand, maybe talking about his mother in a positive light, instead of thinking of her sitting in a cage, would be a good way to redirect his feelings. She wished she knew how to handle situations like these. Give her a knife, sword, or gun, and she was in her element. This stuff was so far out of her element she'd do better to try to fly.

"My mother. She played all the time when I was a kid."

Yep, I'm an asshole. "Um, you play well." *Oh my Gods, what's wrong with me?*

Ben looked up from the fingerboard as his fingers stilled on the strings. Thunderclouds covered his face, and his stare held her mute and unmoving. He set the guitar down on the coffee table and crossed his arms over his chest, and she wished she'd never stopped here. She should've gone back to her room where she belonged. Alone. Where she couldn't do any harm.

"So when were you going to let me in on the secret?" Ben asked.

The not so funny part of that question was the fact that Marie wasn't sure which secret he was talking about. What she'd done in her past, her family's betrayal, the fact that she was universally hated among the clan and pack, or the mate thing. To keep herself from saying something she'd regret—on top of all the other things she regretted—she figured asking him would be the best route.

"What secret are you asking about?"

"Well, at least you didn't try to deny that you have one," Ben replied.

"Everyone has secrets. Don't make it sound like an indictment."

"Fair enough."

"Well, are you going to ask or continue to scowl?" He didn't move, which made her want to leave in a big way, but she knew how he must be torn up about his mother, so she gave it another go. "I'm not a mind reader. You have to ask."

Ben uncrossed his arms and leaned his elbows on his knees, bringing him even closer to her. "How about the one involving me, mate? And, yeah, I know what that is."

"Who told you?"

"Does it matter?"

"No."

"Is that why you've been acting insane for the last few days?"

"Well, I wouldn't say insane, but…uncomfortable," she answered, figuring there was no use avoiding some version of the truth.

He shook his head. "When did you find out?"

"Last night."

"I never figured you to be a human hater, but I guess I was wrong." The disappointment in his voice hurt more than any injury she'd ever received, which made her really hate this mate thing. He shouldn't have that kind of control over her emotions. Actually, he shouldn't have any control over any aspect of her life.

"That's why you've been avoiding me, huh? Couldn't stand to be anywhere near me? Afraid if it got out that you were mated to a hybrid, people might turn their backs on you like my mother's clan did to us."

Marie knew she should remain silent, let him hate her for what he believed was the truth. It would be easier for him if he thought the worst of her. Then, when she put distance between them, the physical component of being mates would be weaker, and he could learn how to get on with his life without having this obligation neither of them wanted hanging over his head.

However, the "mate" part of her couldn't stand his pain. Instinctually, she wanted to soothe him, comfort him, and tell him everything would be all right because she had his back. The thought that she'd be a source of support almost made her laugh. Her standing beside him would put him in the same situation he and his mother had been in: exiled from his clan. She wouldn't and couldn't do that to him. Maybe if he knew the facts, he'd understand why they couldn't be together.

"You're right. I was staying away from you, but not for the reasons you assumed. This has nothing to do with me hating humans. You've seen me with the children. You know that's not true. This is about me and the clan. They turned their backs on me long ago."

He tilted his head as if he was interested. "Go on."

She dreaded the inevitable disgust on Ben's face when he found out what she'd done, but he deserved the truth. Marie never wanted him to think his human half was the cause of their incompatibility, and that being a hybrid made him less than.

"I'm not the bear you think I am." She spoke in measured tones in an attempt to keep her emotions under control. When had what Ben thought become so important to her? "Long story, and unimportant as it pertained to my actions. I had a choice, and I chose to challenge Rose for her position as matriarch of the clan in a battle to the death."

He looked more confused than angry. "You're both still alive."

"Only by the grace of the matriarch. She could have killed me that day. She was within her rights to do it, and she should have. Living as a disgraced bear, an outsider to the clan, someone who's not to be trusted is anathema to a shifter. My clan is my family. The lifeblood for which we live and fight. Being shunned is a slow death, more painful than the blade that Rose should've used to sever my head from my body." Ben looked horrified. "Don't you see? It isn't what the clan would think of me if I were with you that I'm worried about, it's the other way around. For the shifters of this clan to accept you, you can't have an attachment to me."

"Fuck that." The response of a man completely unfamiliar with clan life. "First, tell me why you did it. I've seen you and Rose together. You're friends. There's not anger or hostility between you."

"That's Rose. Good to the core." She sighed. "Listen, it doesn't matter why it happened," she said. "I should have never done it. I betrayed my alpha triad."

"Tell me," he urged while inching closer. "You want me to understand, then I need all the facts." Now she was being interrogated by the police trooper he was trained to be. Damn, he was sexy as hell taking charge. *I'm baring my soul here while picturing him wearing his badge and not much more. He's right. I am insane.*

"It's an ugly story I don't like repeating."

Ben reached out and took hold of her right hand. "Please. For me."

Damn. He's not playing fair. The comfort from that one touch alone raced through her body, leaving a warmth she'd only imagined existed.

She closed her eyes and took a deep breath. Reliving her life story was going to kill. She carried so much pain and guilt, most days she could hardly tolerate being in her own skin. But for Ben, she would try.

"The first thing I remember as a child was isolation. Loneliness. I wasn't permitted to leave the house unless it was for a clan function when attendance was mandatory. My mother homeschooled me, or at least that's what she told people. To this day, I can only read and write at a fifth-grade level, and even then, I'd had to mostly teach myself." When it looked as if Ben was going to say something, Marie shook her head. "If I stop, I may not start again."

He took hold of her other hand before nodding for her to continue, remaining silent, but he wore an encouraging expression.

"As I grew, things remained pretty much the same. It wasn't until my parents began leaving the house in the middle of the night that my life took a more violent turn. If I'd ask them where they were going, I earned a slap to the side of the head as a reminder to mind my own business and remain silent. I was young and didn't know any better. I thought everyone's parents treated them that way."

Ben's grip on her hands tightened.

"One night, foolishly, I followed them into the woods. They traveled for hours in their bear forms, to the point that I wasn't sure we were still in our own territory. I smelled the campfire long before I saw it, and the men with their guns standing around it talking."

Bens eyes narrowed and his lips formed a thin line.

"Instead of avoiding the men, my parents shifted to human form and joined them. I was confused, unsure of what I saw, and too far away to hear what was being said. They were laughing, and plastic cups were being handed around, followed by a bottle of something.

"Even as young as I was, and as sheltered as I had been, I knew that the whole thing, whatever it was, shouldn't be happening. I'd heard the alpha triad tell us how dangerous the human hunters were. I couldn't understand what my parents were doing with them. Somewhere along the line, I must have let my guard down enough for someone to sneak up behind me. The next thing I knew, I was being dragged to the fire. When I looked up at my captor, it was my brother's face I saw."

Damn. She hadn't thought she wanted to talk about this, but once she got going, the floodgates had opened. The emotions these memories were stirring up was making her throat dry and difficult for her to speak. "May I have a glass of water, please?"

"Of course." Ben was up and on his way toward the kitchenette faster then she'd ever seen him move.

When he returned, he handed her the water and set down a box of tissues on the coffee table in front of her. After taking a long refreshing drink, she looked at the box quizzically until Ben motioned toward her eyes. Marie raised her hand and ran her fingertips across her cheek, the resulting tremble had to have been noticeable.

When had she begun crying? Better question: when was the last time she'd actually cried? For the life of her, Marie couldn't remember.

Ben held out the innocuous box, and grudgingly she took a tissue. She wasn't fond of showing weakness, people took advantage of vulnerabilities.

"I swear I never would," Ben said before retaking his position on the couch beside her.

Marie didn't even bother scolding him to stay out of her thoughts. He was her mate, even if she intended to do nothing about it.

"I believe you." What surprised her was she meant it, even though it shocked the hell out of her. She loved Rose and the other goddesses, but she'd never trusted anyone one-hundred-percent. Until now.

"Thank you."

"So, you can imagine how happy my parents were to see me out there in the woods witnessing their meeting. The last thing I remember about that night was the butt end of a rifle coming down on my head. The next day I woke up at home, but I wasn't in my bedroom. I don't know why, or if they'd had plans to use it on someone else, but I was in a cell in the basement of our house. The basement door had always been locked before then, so I never knew what was down there."

She remembered the cold rock walls, cobwebs, and unfinished rafters, but the one thing she could never forget was the dampness. A rusted tap on the far side of her cell dripped a constant stream of water down the rocky wall and into a puddle spanning a quarter of her already spare space.

"I was given a mattress, an old desk with a few of my belongings on it inside a cardboard box, and a pail of water. My first instinct was to take my most precious items and find a place to hide them, which I did by dislodging one of the stones and shoving the few things that were truly mine behind the stone.

"Next was food, but when I made noise to get someone's attention, instead of bringing food to me, I was beaten. I learned quickly never to make a sound and how to survive under the constant threat of being returned to the hunters."

Though he didn't say a word and sat in rapt silence, through their mate link she could feel his blood boiling. What an odd feeling to have someone you barely knew taking up your side with such vehemence.

"It wasn't long after I'd had my first beating that I heard them talking upstairs. They must've left the door ajar by accident. It disgusted me to hear my family celebrating the death of the old alpha triad. They were Mason and Riker's parents, and they had been killed while on a run in the forest. Later, when I was temporarily freed, I'd heard how chaotic everything became after the triad's death. In all the confusion and grief, no one in the clan seemed to notice I was missing."

Before she reached forward to her glass of water, Ben handed it to her and waited for her to finish before taking it back and putting it on the table.

"I remained in the cell full-time as my family systematically created a tool that they could use to get what they wanted. I had no idea what they were capable of, but through the beatings and infrequent food, I learned that if I didn't do as I was told, they'd have no problem letting me starve to death. I'd heard them arguing when my mother was on the way downstairs, and heard Mason and Riker had taken over the leadership of our people.

"If anyone came to ask about me, I had no idea. But I didn't think my absence was noticed since I'd been mostly a ghost to the the clan since my birth."

Ben grimaced, and she knew he was feeling the pain telling the story had dragged up in her body. It'd been a while since she allowed what'd happened to her to seep out of the box she'd put in the corner of her heart. And right now, it hurt worse than while she had been going through it. In reflection, she felt more humiliated than at the time everything was happening because now she could see how she'd been used and manipulated.

"As time went on, my parents began to feed me a bit more, telling me they saw I was trying. Now I know they were brainwashing me, but when you're starving all the time, any food is good food, and any compliment is welcome. When they hinted at a way that I could possibly redeem myself, I would have done anything to let my bear run free out in the sun, never mind the thought of all I could eat and seeing my clan again. They used that need. They used my weaknesses to get what they wanted."

Ben clasped both hands over hers and held on tight. *If you want to stop, I understand.*

Better I finish it. There's not much more to tell.

He nodded.

She took a deep breath and continued. "When they came to me with their idea, I knew they'd finally gone insane. But, I listened in case there was any chance for me to escape. For reasons I didn't know at the time, they wanted me to sneak into the alpha triad's bedroom. I was told that Mason and Riker had found their fated mate, and she was a wolf. My only objective was to scare the wolf away by pretending that I was already the leaders' mistress." She barked out a laugh. "Can you imagine how ludicrous that sounded? Who was I to them?"

If Rose was new, she couldn't've known that.

She nodded. "Well, stupid as it sounded, more importantly, in the back of my mind, I was making plans to escape. When the day came, my parents had yet another surprise for me. I was held down as they implanted a tracker inside my body through a needle. If I tried to flee, they would hunt me down and make me pay for disobeying them."

Ben looked murderous. "Has Jewel removed it?"

"Yeah. A while ago."

"Good." He lifted his chin for Marie to continue.

"When I entered the clan house, I was disoriented. I hadn't been out of my cell in years, and I barely recognized my clan members. I didn't know who I could trust to help me. No one knew me or seemed to care. Everyone was happy and celebrating their new matriarch. Without the ability to run, or anyone who could help me, I followed my instructions and lay in their mating bed, waiting for Rose to find me."

Marie remembered the day clearly. The stars in the sky were so bright, and the fresh air had filled her lungs. For the first time in years she was breathing clean air, and she wanted to shift and roll around in the forest. Even in human form, the feel of the chilly night on her skin was wondrous.

Ben lowered his eyelids and drew in a deep breath through his nose. He felt what she'd remembered. The elation of being free, if even for a moment, had been heaven sent. "What happened when Rose arrived?" he asked.

She couldn't help but laugh. "Of course she saw right through me. Rose didn't believe I was their mistress for a second, and asked me to leave. But before I could, Mason and Riker came running in, and I made a split-second decision."

"To challenge Rose?"

"No. To force the alpha to kill me."

Ben looked at her like she'd grown two noses. "What the hell?"

"It would have been the perfect solution. My parents wouldn't get what they wanted, and I'd be free of them. I knew if the triad sent me back to my family, I'd never be seen alive again. So I made an aggressive move toward the matriarch. Enough to be seen as a threat, which caused Mason to attack to protect his mate."

"But he didn't kill you."

"He would have. His bear was out for blood, and I didn't blame him. I'd done it to get that reaction. It'd been what I'd wanted him to do. What I hadn't expected was Rose stopping him. I didn't know her. I had no idea about her capcity for kindness and forgiveness. I'd thought she'd be fine with getting me out of the way." She shook her head. "You know, I don't even remember uttering the challenge. All I could think of was being sent back to my cell, and I panicked. The last thing I wanted was to be the matriarch of this clan. What I wanted was to be as far away from here as possible."

"If there was a fight, how are you still alive? Not that I'm complaining, but Rose is still matriarch, so she had to have won the battle."

"Yeah, there was no battle. Remember, crazy powerful goddess powers. That was the day Rose discovered she was the reincarnation of the Goddess Thorne, the Huntress. I didn't even try to hurt her. I went to my knees and awaited my death. I wanted it. Nearly begged for it. All I could think was I would finally be free."

"But she chose not to kill you," Ben guessed.

"That was the first time in my life that I was shown compassion. I don't know what she saw in me, but not only didn't she kill me, she refused to send me back to my family. Shortly after, the triad had discovered my family had worked with the human hunters and the hyenas to set into motion the original alpha triad's death years earlier.

"I'm told my mother stabbed my father before killing herself during questioning. They truly deserved one another. My brother was punished by the alpha and beta for his part in the betrayal."

Ben leaned forward and took her into his strong, warm arms. An overwhelming sense of peace surrounded her in safety and allowed her to finally grieve. Her tears flowed for the little girl she'd been, for the familial love she'd been denied, and the guilt she still carried like a yoke around her neck.

He held her closer, dragging her onto his lap, surrounding her with his body, allowing her the time and safety she needed to deal with her wounds and the life she'd been forced to live.

For that alone, Marie would forever be grateful to her mate, even if she couldn't keep him.

Chapter Eight

Ben felt Marie's body go limp in his arms. He couldn't blame her for falling asleep, carrying around that much sorrow and guilt had to be exhausting. With a slight shift in his position, he was able to get his arms underneath her back and knees before carefully lifting her from the couch.

His room was set up like a studio apartment. A screen separated the living room and bedroom, and a short wall divided the small kitchen with its attached bathroom from the living area. It was only a matter of ten steps before he was laying Marie down on his bed. He unlaced her shoes and took them off, and then discarded his own.

Grabbing the blanket from the foot of the bed, he covered her and walked over to the other side of the mattress. There was no way he'd leave her to wake up alone in a strange bed. He crawled in beside her, fully clothed.

He'd like to have believed she trusted him enough to have passed out like that, but he knew her emotional exhaustion had overtaken her. He'd felt her pain and anguish and it exhausted him. He couldn't imagine what she'd lived through. He'd had a mother who'd loved him enough for an entire clan. She knew what she was missing when they cast her out, but he hadn't. He'd been adored, encouraged, and supported. He never doubted how much his mother cared for him.

He lay on his side so that he could finally drink in Marie's beauty. Her ebony hair looked so soft that he was tempted to touch it, but he didn't want to do anything that might wake her, and he knew she'd be pissed if he'd touched her without her consent. He'd daydreamed about what it would feel like to run his fingers through the soft waves, but that would have to wait until she was ready to admit they were going to be together until one of them drew their last breath.

His gaze traveled her face, landing on her lips, which were full and looked entirely too kissable. Well, at least right now when she wasn't pursing them together in anger or frustration. She had light freckles scattered over her straight nose, which made her youthfully endearing. She had no idea how stunning she was. Tall, built—he had no use for scrawny women—and fierce, even without this mate connection, he'd been drawn to her the moment he saw her.

He was beginning to feel like a pervert for watching her while she slept, so he rolled onto his back and stared at the steel-plated ceiling. Besides, he had a whole stack of new information he needed to work through, and now was as good a time as any.

Hope hadn't intended to let the cat out of the bag when she asked him how he was doing with the whole mate thing. To be honest, Ben had been wondering what was going on between him and Marie. Knowing she hadn't discovered the truth herself until the night before helped, but didn't dismiss the fact that she hadn't told him.

Would she have ever told him? All things considered, Ben doubted it. However, it wasn't because of what he'd assumed: that she hated his human side. Instead, he'd learned it'd been something far more horrific. How she'd survived her family's reign of terror was a testament to her strength and fortitude, and her loving spirit. From what he'd seen, she wouldn't believe that about herself, but he'd seen it time and again, especially with the children. It infuriated him that she discounted her worth.

Given what she'd told him, he wasn't surprised she didn't know her value as a member of the clan. While she was a child, she'd had almost no contact with them. When she was imprisoned by her family, no one from the clan had ever come looking for her. It was as if she didn't exist.

Where were the people who had sworn to protect her? If not the alpha and beta, security forces who knew the population and checked on their well-being from time to time to keep a finger on the pulse of the community. Of course, he realized that Mason and Riker had suffered the loss of their parents, the clan's alpha triad, but when you're meant to lead, you had to put that grief aside to make sure each and every member of your clan is safe.

While most of the blame fell at Marie's family's feet, the clan had to own their culpability in allowing those disgusting excuses for parents do what they did to their child. He couldn't wrap his mind around what kind of being would ever do something like that to their own. Monsters came in all shapes, sizes, and names, the most despicable betrayal coming from mom and dad.

Marie's lack of concern for her own life was frightening, but now understandable, albeit completely unacceptable. That behavior had to stop immediately, and he'd make sure of it by showing her how important she really was. Especially to him.

She was out of her mind if she thought he was going to sit back and accept that they couldn't be mates. To hell with anyone who thought his mate deserved to be punished for the rest of her life for what her parents had done. He may not be full bear-shifter, but that had never stopped him before, and now he had someone important to fight for.

If Marie thought that for one moment he was going to let her walk away without a fight, she was in for one hell of a surprise.

***

Marie hadn't been this comfortable in…well, ever. Her thoughts were calm, and her body relaxed. What a heady feeling. Ben's occasional snore confirmed what her body already knew, she was in his bed.

Opening her eyes, she took in her surroundings. According to the digital clock on the bedside table, it was a few minutes past two in the morning. She'd been sleeping for over four hours, and it had been the most restful slumber she'd ever had. Not one nightmare that she could remember.

This mating thing had its serious advantages.

"I'd say there are plenty more advantages from where that came from." Ben's sleep roughened voice did things to her body that were possibly illegal in some states.

With her shifter abilities, she was able to see well in the dark, and enjoyed when his brilliant green eyes opened. He grinned at her. His angry demeanor was a memory as he raised himself up on his elbows to look down at her. "How are you? And don't try to bullshit me."

Only he could make care and concern sound like a order from a commanding officer. "Better, thank you."

"Anytime you need me, I'll be there."

Marie wished that could be true. "Listen, we need to discuss where we go from here."

"Agreed."

"Now you've got to see reason for us to stay apart, after knowing what you now know about me. There's no way we can become mates."

"Become mates? Honey, we're already mates."

"Technically, true, but we don't have to go forward with the full mating. We don't have to exchange the mating bite. No one will ever have to know you had anything to do with me. I was assigned to you, and that's it."

Ben's grin vanished, and his face settled into that stern expression she'd come to know well. "Let's try this again, shall we? I'm not going anywhere without you by my side."

"I don't think you understand what's at risk here." She couldn't allow this to happen.

"Oh, I have a firm grasp on the reality of things. I just don't care." He reached out to touch her hair. "May I touch you?"

Marie knew what her answer should be, but damned if she could make herself say it. "Yes."

He didn't wait for her to change her mind and dove right in, running his fingers through her hair. "I knew it'd be as soft as I imagined."

"You imagined what my hair felt like?"

"I've imagined many things when it comes to you."

"I don't know if I should be flattered or weirded out." She lifted a brow. "No one knows how long we'll be down here or how the whole situation is going to play out. You'll need allies among the clan and packs. Once we get your mother here, I think it will be easier for them to accept you as one of them."

Ben's warm, calloused hand cupped the side of her face, and she allowed herself to lean into it. The pad of his thumb skimmed her bottom lip, and instinctively, she poked her tongue out for a taste of his skin. His appreciative groan only made her want to do it again, but she knew better than to want something she couldn't have. She took tighter control over herself.

"This can't happen."

"Too late. It's happening. You forget I'm used to being an outsider. Too human for the bears, and too bear for the humans,"

Ben said. "I'd rather stay an outsider with you than be inside the clan without you. That's nonnegotiable."

Marie's rational brain fought to stay the course, while the rest of her was slowly leaning closer to the defiant man the gods had chosen for her. The pull was real. Everything about Ben drove her to get closer. From his compassion and concern for others to his sexy-ass grin and his never-surrender attitude. He was the complete package. He ticked all her boxes, and until him she hadn't even known she'd had boxes.

One thing was a for sure: when it came to matching mates, the gods knew what they were doing.

"I don't deserve a fated mate," she whispered, because anything louder might break her heart and the bubble of intimacy surrounding them.

"Neither do I," he replied while bringing his face inches from hers. "Let's be undeserving together."

She had no reply to that. So she did what she'd been yearning to do from the minute she saw him: she closed the distance between their lips. Their first kiss was tentative, but it set off a spark that lit her body on fire with need. By the second kiss, she dove in urgently, demanding more and damn if he didn't deliver.

His hand at the back of her head held her close. He wrapped his free arm around her waist and pressed her body against his. She couldn't imagine being more turned on. While his tongue and mouth devoured hers, his arms and hands cocooned her in safety. It amazed her he had such an overwhelming effect on her.

Her body was no longer her own, and her mind became consumed with thoughts of mating with him. She broke the kiss and asked, "Are you sure?"

He nodded.

"Absolutely sure."

He grinned.

"One-hundred-percent—"

He shut her up by rubbing his thumb across her bottom lip, causing goose bumps to spring up all over her arms. His eyes were impossibly green and brimming with emotion, and his breathing was strained. "I'd be honored if you accepted me as your mate."

Hot damn. Decision made, she began unbuttoning his shirt, stopping partway to run the palms of her hands over his muscular, hairy chest. His skin was hot to the touch, and for a moment, she lost control of herself, extended her claws, and she sliced the remainder of his shirt into pieces.

She ducked her head and said into his chest, "Sorry." *Great time to lose control.*

He lifted her head with a finger under her chin. His eyes took on a darker hue as she watched it happen. "No reason to be sorry. Let me help you with yours." In one swift motion, he took hold of the neckline on her V-neck T-shirt and tore it straight down the center. Now, she'd never been more turned on.

Marie slid her shirt the rest of the way off and tackled Ben to the bed. His responding growl was sexy as hell, and added fuel to the fire burning inside her. She leaned down to take a kiss, but Ben had other ideas, lunging up before rolling her beneath him as he mastered her lips.

He unhooked her bra, and it soon joined what was left of her shirt on the floor.

Glorious. The feel of his chest hair against her sensitive nipples made her moan loud. Soon that skilled mouth of his was working its way down her neck, only stopping to press his teeth into the soft skin where her neck and shoulder met without breaking the surface. It would seem his instincts were well in tune with a full bear-shifter.

She strained to get closer to the sensation, but he continued to move further down her body, only stopping when his hot tongue was circling one of her peaked nipples. After torturing her with teasing nips, he sucked her breast into his warm, wet mouth, sending her into an unexpected orgasm. The rush, so sudden and intense, had her crying out in pleasure.

Somewhere between her euphoric high and returning to reality, her jeans had been slid off, leaving her only in her panties. Ben jumped off the bed and began undoing the button on his waistband while Marie removed the last bit of her clothing. She watched as inch by inch, her mate's pants slid down his muscled legs, leaving him standing in only his boxer briefs.

He reminded her of a redheaded Adonis, lover of Aphrodite, only exceedingly better endowed, and you bet, she was staring.

"You planning on hopping back in here with me?" Marie purred. "Or do I come to you? 'Cause either way, I need us to be skin to skin." A newfound courage had overtaken her, and she acted on it. She knew what she wanted and wasn't afraid to get it.

Ben's responding laughter warmed her even further. This was the man she was destined to spend her life with: all six-foot-four, brave, quirky, resilient, sexy inch of him.

He crawled up from the foot of the bed, leaving no doubt that she was being stalked by the glint in his eyes. A rush ran through her body as she leaned back against the headboard and waited for her man to arrive.

A warm, wet tongue lapped at her calves up to that spot right behind her knees that drove her wild. Marie's sensitive skin quivered at his touch, begging for more. Her moans were playing on a continuous loop, her desire driving her to be one with him.

"Baby, you taste so sweet. I could lick and nibble at you for hours," he crooned before moving onto her thighs.

Nothing in this world could have stopped her from spreading those thighs he was so thoroughly exploring. She wanted to share everything and every part of herself with her mate. She'd never done anything remotely close to this before. In truth, she'd never done anything sexual with anyone.

Ben froze.

What had she done wrong?

"Marie, honey, have you ever made love before?"

Yep, he'd heard her thoughts. *Shit.*

"Um...well...um...not really. I've never been with anyone." Gods, she felt like an idiot. "It wasn't exactly possible in my world."

He crawled the rest of the way up the bed, and she feared the worst. She'd turned her own mate off. The final insult to her insignificant life stung more than any other abuse ever could.

"No. Don't do that," he growled. "You are stunning. Nothing on heaven or earth could make me turn away from you."

"Then why did you stop?"

"Because things were moving too quickly, and I wanted to make sure you were okay with everything," he explained. "This, our mating, is special and shouldn't be rushed."

"Special? Me?"

"Damnit, yes you. I will love up on you until you believe that to be true," he said while cupping her cheek and bringing their lips together for a deep, thorough kiss that left her panting for more.

He retreated back down her body and resumed his exploration of her thighs. *Special.* She was special to Ben. That was all she needed to allow herself to relax back against the pillows and let him have his way with her body.

She may be unskilled at lovemaking, but she was willing to learn, and a quick study.

When Ben licked his way up her thigh and circled her core, Marie surrendered to the rush of need pulsing through her veins. She threw her head back at the first touch of his tongue along her labia. The sensation was unlike anything she'd ever experienced, and she wanted more.

She groaned her approval as her mate dove deeper with every lick. Her back bowed off the bed when his tongue delved deep into her core, bringing her to her second orgasm of the night.

Her mind was spinning. Filled with desire and need, she felt like a leaf in the wind being tossed where the fates would take her. Marie's nipples peaked at the slightest touch and she was desperate for more.

"Ben, please," she moaned.

"Say it again."

"Hmmm?"

"My name on your lips, moan for more. Do it again."

"Ben," she breathed out on a sigh.

He reared up, bringing his body against hers, the head of his cock pressing against her core.

"I love you, Marie. Don't ever doubt that."

"Make love to me, my mate."

Ben pushed forward as her body stretched to his will. The soft skin covering a rod of steel brushed against nerves that had never felt this sensation before, bringing them to life with explosive results.

He stopped, wrapped his arm around her waist and pressed his lips to hers as he surged all the way to the hilt. She felt a twinge of pain as he broke through her innocence.

"Marie, do you accept me as your mate?" Ben asked while holding his body completely still.

"With my whole heart, I accept you as my mate, Trooper Ben Brown."

His responding grin ensured her addition of the honorific to his name had been received with love. Forever he would be known as her Texas State Trooper, and she loved it.

Slowly, with controlled movements, Ben pushed forward, sliding out a little before slipping deep inside of her. The twinge of pain gave way to her body relaxing, and accepting his.

He buried himself deep inside her, claiming her as his own before pulling back. Marie's breathe caught in her throat as her mate began an unhurried pace. His hips thrust forward, pulling the air from her lungs before retreating slowly, pulling out, and acceptance gave way to indescribable moments of bliss.

She loved him. She really loved him. There wasn't one part of her that didn't want him. His zest for life and capacity to believe in another being had brought her further out of her self-imposed isolation.

With every thrust, he pushed her higher. Her body reached out to him and grabbed hold with everything she had. Their bodies molded together in a rhythm that drove her on, reaching for the connection to her mate that would solidify their bond.

Ben ran his hand through her hair and grabbed hold of the nape of her neck. "Our bond is already solid. You are mine, and I am yours forever."

Marie felt his body coil moments before he buried himself deep inside of her. The rush of her orgasm took her under, and she heard her mate cry out as his own release took him over. Then he struck, sinking his new canines into the side of her neck. Moments later, she did the same to him, sealing their bond.

When she floated back down to reality, Marie found herself encased in her mate's arms. Her body satiated by his love.

Could this be what she'd been missing all along? True love. No catches or strings attached.

Could it have been this easy?

Chapter Nine

Bright and early, well, it would have been bright if they'd been aboveground, a much larger force than the original scouting party had assembled to return to the zoo. The mission was simple, if not fraught with complications: free the caged shifters. They knew how extreme the danger was.

In the time they'd spent cataloging the comings and goings around the roadside zoo, a few new bits of information had been gathered. Humans and hyena-shifters were *helping* the Collector Demons. However, their team was unsure if the coconspirators had a choice.

Well over one hundred shifters were being held inside the zoo walls by a group comprised of demons, humans, and hyena-shifters over forty strong. Ben couldn't help but wonder why they were being kept alive. From what he'd learned, Collectors typically killed whatever they came up against.

Marie was across the room, suiting up while having a conversation with Raz, Rose, and Zahra. Ben took the opportunity to ask Mason and Riker a question that had been dogging him since last night.

He walked the few feet over to where they were standing. "Do you have a moment?"

Both looked at him in question. "What's up?"

"I need to know how the leaders of a clan could forget about one of your members."

The two looked at each other before nodding. "I see Marie has opened up to you about her past," Mason said.

"Yeah, but more imporatantly, this." Ben pulled his shirt down far enough for them to see his mating bite.

"Congratulations on your mating," Riker said.

"You're not pissed that I'm only half bear-shifter?"

"No, perhaps curious as to how it's possible, but that's all," Mason replied, and Ben believed him. "As for your original question, what happened to Marie should never have gone unnoticed. I am fully responsible for my part in that, as is my brother. We were lucky to be graced with a mate who would never allow something so heinous to be missed. We are working to become more vigilant so that it never happens again."

"Lucky, absolutely. But that cuts both ways." Rose's voice came from behind him, meaning Marie was sure to be close by.

"What's going on?" Marie asked, and he turned to look at her.

Secrets were not his thing, at least when it came to his loved ones. "I had a few questions for the leaders."

"And as your mate, he has every right to ask them," Mason said, which surprised Ben.

Most men of authority didn't like to be questioned, much less accused of failing at their duty. Ben was reminded why he'd respected the triad almost immediately.

"Then why is she still being mistreated by her fellow shifters?" Ben had to know. No one in their right minds could hold Marie responsible for what happened.

"Simple. The rest do not know the truth," Rose said, and by her tone, this had to have been a hotly contested issue.

"No one needs to know my disgrace," Marie stated. "It doesn't change what I've done."

Ben was beginning to see this on a whole new level, and he didn't like what he saw. "You believe you should continue being punished?"

"This is not the time or the place to have this conversation. Now, if we all could manage to keep the task at hand at the forefront of our minds, we might get out of this alive." Marie had officially slammed the door on any further discussion by walking away.

Ben pivoted around to catch up to his mate. "Hey," he called. She kept walking. "Hey, baby, slow down."

She looked over at him from where she'd stopped to strap on more weapons to her tactical vest with practiced precision. "The alpha is right, as my mate, you have a right to defend me. However, I ask that you leave this one alone, I wish to deal with it my way."

"Okay. But be advised. We're going to revisit this," Ben said. He wrapped his arms around his mate's waist and nuzzled the side of her neck. "I'm not going to ask you to forgive me for wanting everyone to know how awesome you are."

"Has anyone every said, 'Oh, Trooper, you're so sweet?'" He laughed. "I get it. And I kinda like this big, burly bear side of you," she said with a low, evocative come-on tone.

That was when he noticed the room had gone quiet. Both he and Marie looked up to find the assembled team staring at them. Ben felt his mate's body stiffen and could sense her unease. He wouldn't allow it.

"What? Haven't you seen two mates together before?" Ben questioned the entire group. "Get used to it 'cause there's no way we're hiding it." He dared one of them to say a derogatory word about Marie.

Ben felt a rush work its way through his body, but refused to look away from the gathered shifters. At least until his mate looked up at him and gasped.

***

Marie had watched as Ben's eyes turned partially brown last night, but now they were completely black. His canine teeth had extended below his bottom lip, and she was positive she could feel claws on the tips of his hand pressed against her back.

"Ben?" She didn't know quite what to say. Would he be upset about the changes?

"What's wrong, honey?"

"You, um…might want to have a look at yourself," Marie whispered, while pointing to a full-length wall of mirrors on the opposite side of the room. They had installed mirrors in certain places in the bunkers to give the allusion of more space.

He turned, and it was as if the sea had parted by how fast people moved out of his way so that he could get a better look. She could feel her heart pounding its way out of her chest, and her palms were sweaty. Was this the result of their mating? Was he going to shift even further? Questions played on a loop inside her head as she watched her mate move closer to the mirrors.

He brought his hand up to touch his extended canines, and must have noticed his claws because he held them out in front of himself as if trying to get a better look. He flexed his arms, popping the stitches on several seams as he did. Ben was even more significant than his usual girth, with the muscles to match.

Marie quickly looked over at the three goddesses, who were talking amongst themselves and their mates. No help there. This was up to her. She followed her mate until she was standing by his side once more, and took hold of his hand.

"I'm sorry," she said, because sure as anything, this had something to do with her.

Ben turned to face her. "Sorry?" he asked, and she couldn't tell by his voice how this was going to play out, but she was prepared for the yelling to begin.

Which happened seconds later, but not in the way she'd expected. Ben picked her up and spun her around, while laughing his fool head off. *I finally broke him.*

"Not broke by a long shot, baby," he cheered. "This is the best day of my life. Well, the top couple anyway, considering last night tops everything."

"I don't understand." Apparently, she wasn't the only one confused, which was apparent by the looks on the faces of the gathered team.

"I'm a bear."

"I knew that."

"Now, I can feel it. Since finding out my mother was a bear-shifter, I'd hoped that maybe someday, even though the chance was slim and I'd need a miracle, I'd be able to shift like her."

"Honey, I hate to point out the obvious, but you're not fully shifted." Damn, she wished she could turn off her candor. She was sure that wasn't what he needed to hear right now.

"I know, but someday it could happen, and if not, I don't care. Even having a small part of what it feels like to be a bear-shifter is more than I believed possible. You are my miracle, baby."

Miracle? That'd be a first.

"Let me get this straight, you want to be a bear?" John asked.

"Every day, since I knew it was possible," he answered. "Now, thanks to my mate, I've been given a taste of it. Thank you, honey."

"This might have nothing to do with me," she said. "It may have happened with or without me."

"There's the self-effacing bear I know, but I'm positive this has something to do with our mating."

"He could be right," Jewel said, causing the hum of whispered conversations among the assembled to raise significantly. "The exchange of DNA when giving the mating bite may have been the catalyst. I'll have to perform a couple tests to be sure."

"I do not want to rain on this parade, but we still have a mission to complete if we want to arrive under cover of darkness," Axel, the wolf alpha, stated. "We can discuss this when we get those people back to safety."

Marie jumped down out of Ben's arms, and readjusted her sword. "Right. Sorry. Let's go."

"Again, nothing to be sorry about. I'm amazed by this turn, but we're on a short clock."

Marie nodded, and the team went about final preparations. She pulled Ben to the side, having to make sure he was honestly okay with this. When he ran his claws up and down the backs of her arms, she almost lost track of what she wanted to say. Gods could he get any sexier?

"Are you sure you're okay with this?" Marie ran the tip of her index finger along one of his sharp canines. They weren't excessive, but they were definitely the teeth of a bear.

"Oh, yeah." He grinned. "Completely happy. Who knows, I might shift back or all the way into a bear. It doesn't matter, because at this moment I can feel my bear within me. That's all I've ever wanted."

She looked at his eyes, and she had to admit he did seem excited about it. "Okay, then go get yourself a proper-fitting shirt, and let's go get your mom."

Chapter Ten

They materialized a lot closer to the zoo this time. They'd arrived when the sky was pitch black, and the sun was hours away from rising. Marie stayed low to the ground as she scouted ahead, and at least this time, Ben stayed back with their forces. This trip, they weren't in his familiar woods heading toward a small cave. They were about to attack a Collector facility full of the freaky demons, humans with guns, and hyenas.

Completely different ball game.

She was good at her job. Years spent making herself invisible was coming in handy now. With every move she made, she sent the information back to the team. Which path not to take, possible traps, guard locations. Really, anything she saw was playing like a movie for those waiting behind her.

Two of the goddesses, Raz and Rose, had come along with the team to provide the power needed to get out of here after they'd released the prisoners. Their powers were impressive but exhaustible. If they went in, goddesses ablaze, it was likely neither would have enough strength to dematerialize the entire group of shifters.

The plan was that they'd get into the zoo, unlock the cages, and then wait for the planned distraction to go off before heading for the hills.

The approach from the east appeared to provide the most cover, lodged between old buildings, burnt-out vehicles, and rock formations. When she was within one hundred yards of the fence, Marie stopped and did a more thorough recon of the area before carrying on.

Human guards were posted on each corner, rifles at the ready, while the odd hyena-shifter walked the perimeter. She couldn't help but wonder where the Collectors were hiding out. The team was on the move behind her, so Marie waited until the next hyena turned the back corner before coming out of her hiding spot. A few locations along the fencing were at least partially hidden from view. She didn't expect the humans to go lurking into any dark corners after having met their new masters and found that there were bigger monsters out there than mere shifters.

The humans looked about as alert as lizards lying in the sun. Unless something serious occurred, they weren't moving, making it a lot easier for her to cut her way through the chained linked fences. Once she'd made a substantial hole, big enough for everyone to get through and then back out again, she took her bolt cutters and headed for the first rows of cages.

The first few were empty, making her wonder if they'd held a shifter at one time, but the third contained a flock of hawks. As softly as possible, she said, "We're here to free you. Wait for the fireworks to start, and then open your cages and run due east toward the old Chevy dealership. There'll be shifters waiting to take you to safety."

The padlock fell to the ground, and she was about to go on to the next cell when she remembered something. "If Timothy's family is in there, know that he is safe far away from here." A few of the hawks jumped to a branch closer to where she was standing. This had to be them. "I'll take you to him once we get everyone out of here. I promise."

Marie couldn't remain too long. She kicked the cut lock under a pail so that if a guard came by, they wouldn't notice anything out of the ordinary, and then headed on to the next shifter. Thankfully, the prisoners remained quiet as she moved along and repeated the process dozens of times over.

She'd had to hide a few times when a human or hyena-shifter went by, but luckily with all the various shifter scents in such a confined place, her scent didn't stand out to the shifter traders.

She signaled when most of the cages were unlocked, and members of the team began working their way through the shadows. All of them kept up a constant flow of communication through their shared links. If something went wrong, they would all know about it.

The rusted bars holding the various shifters brought back painful memories, but she shoved them aside so she could carry on. She was free and she was going to do everything in her power to make sure all these shifters were freed. Various feline shifters, birds of all species, wolves, an angry anaconda, a buffalo, deer, and more were housed here. But why? She was sure they'd be able to get more information once they were back in the bunkers. They'd have to wait to uncover the truth.

Her mate quickly caught up with her and watched over her while she continued to cut through the locks. The concerning part was they'd yet to find a bear among them.

They quickly backed into a dark corner when they heard a scratchy voice coming from ahead. Marie leaned right so that she could see farther down the row, and found a male human standing outside a smaller cage.

"You're getting what you deserve animal," he slurred. Was he drunk? "All you had to do was play by the rules, but from what I hear, you never really did from the start."

"Who the hell is he talking to?" Ben asked, but no matter how far she stretched, Marie couldn't see inside the cage.

"I have no idea."

The sizzle was their only warning before whoever was in that cage howled in pain. Sadly, Marie knew the sound of a cattle prod when she heard one.

"Cry, bitch," he laughed. "You should have betrayed your fellow beasts like the rest of your kind have." Another sizzle was followed by a pained howl that faded into a whimper.

That was all Marie could take of this torture, and by her mate's growl, he agreed. Damned if it might raise the alarm.

"I'm going to tear him to shreds."

They inched out of their hiding spot while staying to the shadows as much as they could. When they were only a dozen or so feet away from the degenerate, Joseph, the wolf-shifter who'd apologized to Marie, came racing around the corner.

Joseph didn't even break stride as he wrapped his arms around the asshole's head and shoulders before twisting sharply. The abuser was dead before he ever knew he was in danger. The cattle prod hit the ground at the same time as his body.

Though Marie was shocked by how fast Joseph had responded, she ran the remaining distance to check on the shifter in the cage. Both she and Ben came to an abrupt stop when they found an albino striped hyena chained to the floor of her cage.

Even though she was a hyena-shifter, a traitor to all shifters, Marie's heart went out to her. She understood the look of fear in the hyena's eyes, recognized the scars, and how her body trembled even in her animal form.

"Cut the locks," Joseph demanded. "We have to get her out of there."

Marie didn't think twice and used the bolt cutters like scissors, cutting the wounded hyena from her chains. The woman didn't make a sound but never took her eyes off of Joseph. Ben remained several feet back, watching for any guards that might have heard the ruckus.

Once she managed to get the hyena free, Joseph stepped into the cage and lifted her from the concrete pad. The metal shackle around the hyena's neck would have to be removed once they were all safely back home.

Marie took a step toward the shifter, but quickly moved back when Joseph growled at her. "No one will hurt her."

"I wasn't going to hurt anyone," Marie said, understanding the man's concern. Hyenas weren't widely loved in the shifter community because of their willingness to work with the human hunters. "Joseph, do you know her?"

"No, but I will protect her."

There wasn't any time to figure this all out. "Take the hyena back to the goddesses so she can be taken to safety. Ben and I will carry on here."

Joseph nodded, and for the first time, the woman in question turned her sorrowful, pale eyes on Marie. The exchange took only a moment, but in that time, Marie felt those familiar emotions once again: fear, self-loathing, and loss, but this time they weren't hers, they belonged to this poor abused hyena.

In the distance, Marie could hear vehicles approaching. They were running out of time. Joseph carried the hyena away while Marie and Ben moved impossibly faster. If the shifters were free of their cages, they'd stand a fighting chance. Ben led the way, his semiautomatic up and at the ready. They turned corner after corner, cutting every lock they could find until they came upon a row of larger cages set at the back corner.

As she neared them, Marie had a sinking suspicion they'd found even larger shifters, and perhaps Ben's mother would be among their numbers. The first cage they came upon held a polar bear-shifter, then two alligators, and a mustang. When they came to the next, Ben's body began to vibrate. They'd found who'd they'd been looking for.

"Mom," he called, while reaching his arm through the bars. The bear inside didn't appear to be well. Raising her big grizzly bear head took what seemed to be a great deal of effort, and she looked at Ben. The remainder of her body remained eerily still. "Don't worry, we'll get you out of there."

If Joan had noticed her son's changed appearance, she gave no indication. Marie wasn't even sure the bear was conscious enough to realize they were real. She went to work on the padlocks as headlights cast their glow from the front of the facility. Yep, they were out of time, all right.

Warnings were coming across the link fast and furious. The planned distraction was on its way to its location, and it was time to go. The moment the last lock hit the ground, Ben ran inside the cage and to his mother's side.

"We have to get you out of here now," Ben said as he ran his fingers through her fur. "Mom, you'll have to shift for me to be able to carry you."

For a moment, Marie thought the big bear wasn't going to do it, but then she realized Joan was so weak it was taking her longer to shift.

Marie grabbed the gun from her back and took up a defensive position in case they were forced to stay and fight. Reports coming in over the link told them every cage found had been unlocked, and in only a few moments, literal fireworks were about to go off.

She looked up at the star-filled sky, waiting for the first signs of the incoming wave. A movement behind her caught her attention, and she glanced back to see Ben carrying a woman out of the cage.

"We have to go," Ben said.

"I'm right behind you," Marie agreed.

In the surrounding silence, a low hum became progressively louder by the second. The team's distraction had arrived on shifter wings. Birds of all shapes and sizes began appearing above the zoo, with the help of Zahra back at the bunkers. They flew in, dropped their devices, and vanished. The small spheres rained down over the zoo, and in seconds, the party was about to begin.

The first set went off spectacularly. Fireworks, smoke, loud bangs, the whole gambit except for one thing, the devices weren't lethal. They couldn't risk injuring the shifters, so the spheres made a lot of noise and threw off a ton of smoke to help shield their getaway without risking any of the good guys.

Everything was going up around them. Cages were thrown open, and the freed shifters made their way to the hole in the fence and freedom. She could hear gunshots peppered in between the fireworks and prayed that none of the prisoners or rescuers were hurt.

Ben bent his body over top of his mother in an attempt to protect her from any stray bullets. Up ahead, the mustang they'd freed was carrying three smaller shifters on his back as it raced away into the darkness. Shifters of every kind flowed through the hole in the fence she'd made, and Marie glanced back to ensure she couldn't see anyone left in the cages. When she turned back, it was just in time to spot a hunter lining Ben up in his sites from his perch on top of a pen.

Using her shifter speed, Marie raised her weapon and fired off one round straight into the center of the human's forehead before he could pull the trigger. They were only yards away from the fence line when a hyena raced out from the shadows and took Ben and his mother to the ground.

Without thought, Marie shifted into her bear midstride, and tore the hyena from Ben's back. With her massive paw, she backhanded the traitor into the side of one of the empty cages. Using her big body, she kept a barrier between the hyena and her mate and his mother. She looked back to confirm Ben was up and already lifting Joan back into his arms.

The hyena got up on four wobbly legs, ready for another round.

Marie looked into her mate's dark eyes and said. *"Go."*

"I'm not leaving without you."

"You think a minor hyena can take me on, mate?" she teased, desperate to convince him to leave. *"I'll be done with him and caught up with you before you even reach the rendezvous point."*

He looked unsure.

"Go. I can't fight and protect you and your mom at the same time."

"You'll be right behind me?"

"You bet those sexy canines of yours, I will."

"I love you."

Words she'd never thought would be spoken to her. *"I love you, too."*

Marie turned her attention back to the hyena, who was pawing at the ground in anger before lunging toward her. She rose onto her back legs and towered over the other shifter, but that wasn't enough to make him run in the other direction. Seriously, bad idea.

This time she used her claws when it tried to jump on her back. Blood flowed from the hyena's side before she batted him back out of the way, allowing the last few remaining shifters to make a break for the hole.

Explosions rang out like a symphony of destruction as the sky lit in various colors, and smoke hung heavy in the air. A second growl came from behind Marie and then a third. The hyena's friends were showing up fast, and she had to get out of there.

Marie quickly batted one hyena away when another bit into her back leg, causing her to roar in anger and pain. This one she was going flatten. When she turned to face him, Marie was suddenly confronted with a bigger problem. Collector demons.

***

Ben raced ahead with his unconscious mother in his arms. Shifters were fleeing all around him, and he could see the waiting triads up ahead. Groups of shifters were disappearing as the goddesses transported them to safety before coming back for more. Thankfully, there weren't many of the imprisoned people left to transport back, meaning most were already safe.

By the time he reached them, only a handful had remained. Ben turned to check on Marie only to find dozens of hunters and Collectors headed their way.

"We have to go," Xander shouted, bringing the group together.

Ben motioned for the beta to take his mother. "I have to go back for Marie, she was holding off a hyena so the rest of us could get out."

Bullets began riddling the ground not far in front of them as the enemy got closer.

"Join hands," Rose said and, at the last possible second, took hold of Ben's wrist. "I'm sorry."

Even though he fought to be released, it was too late, and in the next moment, Ben's eyes took in the gray metal walls of the infirmary.

"No," he yelled.

Chapter Eleven

The din of the truck's engine was beginning to pick away at her last nerve. Marie had been in the modified horse trailer for hours, and the noonday sun was high above them. She'd been chained to the trailer bed by her neck and legs, as well as muzzled with a thick steel cage tied at the back of her bear's head.

She'd tugged on the chains so hard that the metal shackles had worn through her thick fur and dug into her flesh, leaving blood staining her legs. Three large hyenas sat staring at her from their positions at the front of the trailer, while two armed humans stood at the back. She'd noticed both had a small red circle tattooed on their necks. Or at least she thought they may have been tattooed.

No matter how hard or often Marie tried, she couldn't reach Ben or the clan. Surely the result of the Collectors somehow severing her connection. The bastards were in vehicles in front of and behind the trailer, each with a human driver. The demons she'd seen back at the zoo were far more advanced than the ones she'd met months ago. These ones seemed to be less "squishy." In previous attacks, she'd seen substantial decomposition of the surrogate bodies. Now there was hardly a scratch on them.

One of the human hunters had the nerve to smirk at her, his superiority unchecked, but little did he know he'd ventured a little too close. Marie lunged forward, reaching far enough to knock the rifle out of the hunter's hands with her muzzle and sending him to the ground. The hyenas didn't even bother to move, and the second man laughed as his partner crab-walked to the farthest corner. The strong scent of urine confirmed she'd gotten her point across.

"Jesus, man. Grow some balls. She can't hurt you," the second man said, before spitting chewing tobacco onto the floor in front of her. "Ain't nothing but demon food now."

Demon food? Marie wondered what the hell he meant by that. Collectors didn't actually consume food, unless you considered humans as a meal. When they took over a body, they sucked it dry before moving on to the next. They couldn't do the same with a shifter, making his statement all the more confusing.

Where are we going? If they wanted her dead, they'd already have done it. So, what did they want from her?

It appeared she didn't have to wait any longer to find out, as the truck slowed and turned onto a long gravel driveway. Marie strained her neck out the small dirt-encrusted windows to see what looked like a processing facility, then she saw the sign.

Johnston's Meat-Packers. *Shit.*

***

Ben paced back and forth, from one end of the infirmary to the other. His mom had been stabilized and was now resting, but his mate was nowhere to be found. He and the goddesses had tried reaching out to her, but hit a wall every time.

Somehow, the Collectors had found a way to disrupt the link, even between mates. Now that Ben could feel his bear, the urgency with which it was clawing to get out was a bit overwhelming. The instinct to hunt down his mate was compelling him to leave now. It didn't matter that he didn't know where she was, he had to get to her, no matter what. While his human brain tried to come up with a plan to rescue her, his bear was furious. He was taking too long.

The double doors leading into the ward opened, revealing both triads, along with Zahra and John.

Ben didn't wait for them to reach him, he ran to them. "Any word on Marie?" He could see by the looks on their faces the news wasn't good.

"We've tried everything we could think of. Even reaching out to the gods hasn't helped. It's as if their intentionally being silent," Raz said as she snuggled her daughter, Asta, tighter against her chest.

"Son?" his mother's weak voice called out from behind him. "Where am I?"

Ben raced to her side, and took hold of her cold, frail hand. "Mom, you're safe."

"Hello, Joan Brown. Welcome to your new home," Mason said in a warm, welcoming voice.

Joan reared back. "We're among a clan?" she asked. "We can't stay here." As suddenly as she'd begun talking, his mother stopped and stared at Ben. "What happened to you?"

Ben smiled for the first time in hours. "I found my fated mate, Mom. Her name is Marie. She's a bear-shifter here among the Porda Clan."

His mother looked confused. "A fated mate brought out more of your bear? Where is she?" The mood changed drastically in the room, and his mother must have noticed. "What's wrong?"

"She's been captured by the Collectors."

His mother looked at him even more shrewdly. "Saving me?" When he didn't answer, she continued, "You saved me but lost your mate. What the hell are you standing around here for, go get her. Those creatures will suck her dry."

"We've lost our link with her, and what do mean 'suck her dry,' ma'am?" Rose asked as she came closer to the bed. "They can only infect humans."

"They've found a way. Smaller shifters die too quickly, but the bigger ones, the stronger ones they can use as a personal power source repeatedly."

Ben was floored. "They're going to use my mate to make them stronger?"

"Yes," she replied. "That's why you found me so weak."

"They did the amplification to you?" Zahra asked.

"Once a week I was transported to a large building, I think it was located on a farm or something because I could hear cows every time the trailer stopped. All I remember after that was a bright light, pain, and exhaustion."

"Any idea how far away from the zoo you were driven?" Ben asked. Maybe they could extrapolate a location using that, and send teams out to sites that fit the bill.

His mother sat quietly with her eyes closed, no doubt trying to remember any detail she could. Ben's body was strung tight, his bear pushing forward, waiting on the answer. This could be their only hope.

She opened her eyes, and he knew the answer before she spoke the words. "No. I'm so sorry. Everything is a blur in my mind." Her eyes filled with tears.

Ben leaned over and gathered her into his arms. "It's okay, Mom. We'll find her." He didn't know how, but he would not lose the woman he loved.

The pain of being away from his mate was an ache in his soul. Emotionally and physically, he was falling apart. He couldn't allow that to happen. Marie was counting on him to get her out of there.

"I found it, thank the gods, I've found it," Jewel hollered, as she ran into the room holding a small shoebox in her hands. "We need to fix it."

Riker went to his sister and asked, "What are you talking about?"

"This," she replied while holding out the box to him.

Ben watched as Riker took the lid off the shoebox and looked inside. "Electronic pieces?"

Ben's heart plummeted, how could those help?

"Yes. Remember when I removed the tracker from Marie, the one her parents had implanted into her?"

"Yes."

"Well, I couldn't get it out. Marie's parents wanted to make sure she never got away."

"This is a story I'll have to hear someday," his mother said.

"But Marie told me that you did remove it," Ben said.

"I lied to her," Jewel admitted. "She was so upset by it, and wanted all memory of her family's perfidy destroyed. When I couldn't get it out, I couldn't break her heart and tell her the truth, so I told her it had been removed, and she never had to worry about it again. This is the locator to find her. I took it apart so that no one could ever use it, but something inside told me not to incinerate it."

Ben released his mother's hand and headed to the box. "How long will it take to rebuild?"

"That's the thing." Jewel frowned. "I wasn't exactly paying attention to what I was doing when I dismantled it. I never thought I'd have to put it back together again."

Ben took the box to get a better look at the parts.

"You can do it, son. I know you can."

"Do what?" Raz asked.

"My son has an innate ability to fix anything mechanical. I can't tell you how many times he tore my home computer apart, simply to see how it worked, and then he'd put it back together like brand new. Ben was seven at the time."

"Do you think you can put it back together?" Jewel asked.

"You bet I'm going to try," Ben replied. "I need tools."

"Follow me," John said.

Before leaving, Ben bent down to kiss his mother on her forehead. "I love you, Mom."

"You are my starlight, Ben."

Ben hadn't heard that term in years. His mother used to call him starlight when he was a child. The memories strengthened his spirit.

He could do this.

He would do this.

***

Joseph set the plate of baked chicken down on the coffee table in front of the hyena lying on the floor in the corner of his living room. He'd set down thick blankets for her to lay upon, but she hadn't made a move toward them.

"Please eat the chicken, little one," he begged. "I heard your stomach growling earlier. I swear it's safe." Joseph picked up a drumstick and took a bite out of it to reassure her.

Unfortunately, she lowered her head to her front paws without giving the chicken a second look. He thought about lifting her up and placing her on the blankets, but a knock on his door stopped him. Her body began to tremble at the sound.

"No one will hurt you. I promise you are safe with me." Slowly, he set his hand on one of her paws. "I will protect you."

The knock sounded again, and he couldn't help but growl, making her pull her paw back. "No, no, no. I was growling at whoever is at our door, not you, never you."

She seemed to calm a bit, and he took that as a good sign. He stood and quickly walked to the door so that whoever it was wouldn't knock again. With a bit more force than necessary, Joseph opened his door to find a pissed-off bear in his face.

"Were you growling at us?" John asked, and Joseph could see Zahra peeking around from behind John's shoulders. *Shit.*

"Yes. No. Not you specifically. You scared my hyena when I was trying to convince her to eat."

"Yes, your hyena," John said, without even trying to hide the disgust from his voice.

Before Joseph had the chance to respond, the big bear-shifter was shoved aside by Zahra. *"That is no tone to use with our guest."*

John had the decency to look a bit ashamed before Zahra took over. *"I apologize for our unannounced visit, but I believe it is imperative to have a word with her."*

"Yes, Goddess. But please go slow. She's terrified."

"Of course."

Joseph stepped aside and allowed the two into his room. The hyena-shifter took one look at the pair and ran to the farthest corner away, trying to make herself as small as possible. It broke Joseph's heart to feel her fear. He went to her, but as he leaned down to reassure her, the entire room was enveloped in comfort and calm.

He looked back to find Zahra's hands glowing with the Eye of Ra. She was using her powers to calm his hyena.

"Little one, Zahra won't hurt you. She's a goddess here to help you." He hoped he wasn't lying because there would be no other option. Joseph would take his hyena to the surface and leave with her if it came down to it.

The goddess stepped closer to them, before coming to sit on the floor beside them. *"Hello, my name is Zahra."*

The hyena became frantic, and Joseph had no other choice but to pull her into the safety of his arms.

"Yes, I can speak to you through your link," Zahra confirmed, and Joseph kicked himself for not explaining that to her earlier. Zahra pulled her hair aside to reveal her scars. *"My real voice was taken from me, but the gods saw fit to restore my ability to speak with others in this way."*

The hyena calmed slightly, but Joseph refused to return her to the hard floor. Instead, he tucked her against his chest, her head lying under his chin.

"As you know, hyenas have not been the friends of other shifters, and that's why I'm here." Before the poor hyena could get too worked up, Zahra carried on. *"You're not in any danger, but you have to understand many have concerns. May I look back in your memories to confirm you aren't a threat to our people? I will need to touch you."*

Joseph knew the other shifters wouldn't take kindly to having a hyena-shifter in the mix, even if she had been a prisoner along with the rest. After a few tense moments, the hyena lowered her head to Zahra.

"Thank you for trusting me," Zahra said, and then placed her hands on the top of the hyena's head.

Time seemed to stretch on too long, but Joseph never took his eyes off the hyena's pure white head.

When Zahra opened her eyes, they were filled with tears, and soon John was at her side. *"Thank you. Now I must ask you one more thing. Do you know where the shifters are taken when they leave the zoo? One of ours was taken during the rescue, and we need to find her."*

"She's the one that cut the locks and chains from you," Joseph explained, hoping to give his hyena a better description of who they were discussing.

Suddenly, out of nowhere, an image slammed into his mind. "Johnston's Meat-Packers." Both Zahra and John looked up at him in question. "The image of a white sign with blue lettering just came to me."

"Is this the place they might have taken her?"

With a bow of the hyena's head, they had their answer. The question of how she put the image into his head would have to wait.

"Can you understand her?" Joseph asked Zahra. "Maybe ask her what her name is?"

Zahra turned her attention back to the hyena. *"Shame? That's what they called you?"*

"To hell with that," Joseph growled, only remembering at the last moment that his hyena didn't like that. "Easy, easy, I'm not upset with you, only that they dared to name you that. You are no one's shame."

"We'll leave you two alone for now," John said. "However, I believe it will be safest if the two of you move into the restricted area until everyone has a better chance to get to know your friend here."

Joseph nodded. If it would be safer for her, then he'd move from the pack.

"You are safe here with us," Zahra said while running her hand over the hyena's white fur. *"You are no threat. I will make sure they know. Raz and her mates will be by later, after we've gotten Marie back. They are the alpha triad of the wolves and are very kind."*

John helped Zahra to her feet and led her out of Joseph's room, closing the door behind them. The hyena jumped out of his arms and onto the floor once again, but he wasn't going to push her.

"So, let's pick your new name." That got her attention. "I've always found Harriett to be a pretty name." If he didn't know better, he'd have sworn she rolled her eyes. "Okay, maybe not. How about Sarah?" That had been his mother's name.

Her ears perked up.

"Sarah, you like Sarah?" With a slight wag of her tail, he had his answer. "Sarah, it is. Well, Sarah, it's nice to meet you. My name is Joseph."

Her head came up off her front paws to stare at him for a moment, before she stood and walked over to the plate of chicken. She took a tentative first bite, and he could hear her stomach growl even louder. With one final look back at him, she finally dove into the plated goodness with gusto, proving how hungry she'd really been.

Sarah wouldn't ever be hungry again.

Joseph sat on the floor, watching as his newly named Sarah finished the chicken, before curling up on the blankets he'd set out for her.

Now he could finally take a deep breath.

Chapter Twelve

If she wasn't afraid before, she was undoubtedly terrified by what she saw now. Shifters of every shape and size either dead or in the process of dying. Cages stacked on top of cages covered an entire wall.

Large hooks hung from a conveyer that snaked across the ceiling as dim lights flickered in and out. Waves of heat wafted up off the concrete in languid tendrils, evaporating back into the air. The stench was unbearable, and it became apparent they'd been operating this facility for a while. How had they not known? Why hadn't the gods told them about it? How many shifters could have been saved from this fate?

Her paws squished against the ground as she walked down one of the side hallways away from the main area, but there was no way in hell she was looking down to see what it was. Marie could hear men and women laughing from another part of the facility, and screams from the other side. This was a real live house of horrors, not some sort of commercialized Halloween version of it.

Marie raged against her restraints, but her body wouldn't obey her. Before they'd removed her from the trailer, they'd placed an electrified collar around her neck, but instead of shocking her as she'd expected it to, it forced her to obey their commands. She'd never thought this type of technology existed beyond sci-fi movies, and wondered where the Collectors were getting them. It certainly wasn't from their he-haw hunters.

A large cage stood at the end of the hall, and she had the sinking feeling that it was waiting for her.

"Get in, beast." The same guy with the chewing tobacco grunted before shoving her into the cage with the sole of his boot. "Now sit." She had no choice but to obey and sat. "Now, stay." He laughed. "Not so scary now, are you? Damn, we should have had these things from the beginning. It would have been a helluva lot easier exterminating the world of these things."

"For your sake, you are fortunate they hadn't been exterminated, because there'd be no use to keep you around, human," a deep male voice said from behind the hunters, but out of her view.

The group parted, allowing a tall, dark-haired man to walk through. Marie had to take a double take to make sure she wasn't seeing things, because she was sure Hollywood heartthrob, Jake Russo, was standing right in front of her. The actor's much-lauded blue eyes had turned oily black, proof of the demon inhabiting the body. There wasn't a mark on him. No degradation of the body, no stiffness or decomposition. Hell, even his coloring was spot on: California tanned.

"You like?" it asked as it ran its hands up and down his suit-clad body. "I searched long and hard for a suitable host. I believe I've chosen well. Call me Russo."

Marie was sure she had to be hallucinating. A demon wasn't only preening in front of her, he was engaging her like a person. Maybe they'd tranquilized her at the zoo, and this was all a bad dream.

"I'm told that you are one of the shifters responsible for freeing some of my stock."

Stock? As in livestock? This shit just kept getting worse by the moment.

"Yet you chose to stay and fight, instead of running like the rest. You're either brave or an idiot. We shall see. In the mean time, I don't want you to worry about my loss. I'm fortunate to have many holding facilities across this dimension, or as you call it, Earth. We'll be restocked within days."

Damnit. Everything inside her wanted to lung forward and rip his throat out, but Marie still couldn't move. If it was the last thing she did, she would make sure this demon would be destroyed.

"Bring her up for the first round of treatments at ten tonight," Russo ordered the others. "And do take care she remains in good health until then, we wouldn't want to waste any of it."

"Yes, boss," tobacco guy responded with a tinge of fear in his voice. Marie knew he should be showing a lot more respect to appease the demon, but he was too stupid to see the threat directly in front of him.

"Not you," Russo said while removing the rifle from the man's hands. "We need to have a discussion." Impossibly fast, Russo used his nails to slash across the man's neck. Not deep enough to kill, but to damage that red circle tattoo. "Bring him."

The other hunters turned on their comrade without hesitation. Her cage door was shut and locked, and they dragged the hollering man away. She should have found some sort of satisfaction in the fact that a hunter, who'd undoubtedly killed other shifters, would get what he had coming to him, but knowing the fate that awaited him, she couldn't.

A portion of the human population was being used to carry out labor for the Collectors. How could they say no? Either you did what you were told, or a demon would simply take over your body. The end. Good-bye. Even if you did try to fight back and killed one of them, they would simply return to vapor and take your body as their new host. A lose-lose if she ever saw one.

What she really needed answers for was why. Why would the Collectors use humans to capture and guard shifters? Why did the demons want live shifters? In the past, they couldn't get rid of shifters fast enough, considering that they couldn't be taken over by the Collectors.

Everything was out of whack, and she found she had way too many questions without answers, and less time with each passing second to find them.

"Ben, please hear me."

***

Ben set the last circuit in place and turned on the tracker. The screen flickered to life, and a few seconds later, GPS coordinates began flashing on the screen.

"I got her," he yelled. "I have her location."

The triads gathered around him. "The teams are ready. Will that give us an exact location when we're on the ground, in case it's a large area?" Rose asked.

"It should," Ben replied. "Once we're anywhere near her, I'll find my mate with or without the tracker."

"Done, let's move," Axel ordered.

As they headed for the door of the equipment bay, Zahra and John came running in. "We have the name of a place from the rescued hyena. Johnston's Meat-Packers."

Ben's heart fell. "Meat-packers?" What were they doing at a meat-packaging facility? Every possibility raced through his mind at once.

"We have to look up the location," John stated.

"I have it," Ben said while holding out the beeping tracker.

"Then let's gear up and get our clan member back," Mason said before rushing out of the door.

Marie, I'm coming for you. Hold on. I will find you.

***

"Psst...psst."

Marie struggled to turn her head in the direction of the noise to find an old man waving at her. He must have shifted to talk to her.

"Don't fight it," he whispered.

Don't fight what? With this collar on, she couldn't raise a claw without permission.

"The machine." He began rocking back and forth in his cage, and she wondered how long the poor man had been trapped here.

What machine?

"The one they use to pull the life from us."

Holy shit.

"If you don't fight it, there won't be so much pain. You have to relax. It won't last long, and then they'll bring you back to your cage and feed you."

Why are they doing this?

Before he could answer, footsteps could be heard coming down the hallway toward them. When Marie turned back to the old man, she found a warthog staring back at her. She'd never met a warthog before.

She could make out three people walking in their direction. *I guess I'll be seeing that machine sooner rather than later.* But to her shock, they walked on by her cage and up to the warthogs.

Marie struggled to move, to somehow stop them from taking the old man, but nothing helped. The damned collar held her in place no matter what she tried. The warthog didn't even fight the hunters as they collared him. It was as if he'd given up on his own life, and simply wanted to help her in some way.

She fought all the more for him but to no avail, and watched as they walked the shifter away. How would he survive whatever they were doing to him? He'd looked so frail in his human form that Marie had her doubts. Maybe to him, it would be a blessing to be taken away from this world and to be finally given peace.

Sitting there waiting was the hardest part. Other than the occasional howl or growl, the area fell into silence, and by the dark sky she could see through tiny windows close to the ceiling, it was night. She wondered if her mate was safe, along with his mother.

Marie didn't even know how many they managed to free, but if she'd saved one shifter from this fate, she'd accomplished something with a life that had mostly been thrown away by her parents. If only she'd known how much life was worth living, she'd have done more. Now that she had Ben, she may have been happy for the first time in her life, and boom, that was gone before it really ever started.

A constant dripping held her attention, and she began counting the drops. When she reached five hundred and sixty-four, they came for her.

Her time had well and truly run out.

Chapter Thirteen

All three goddesses came along for this fight. They were going to hit hard and fast. Ben's only mission was to find his mate and get her out of there. Everyone else would storm the building to find any other shifters that could be trapped in there and take out as many enemies as possible. Whoever got in the way of him finding his mate had better be ready to meet their maker because no one was stopping him.

Teams were being brought in all around the facility so that when they attacked at the same time, the opposing forces would have to stretch their resources to fight them off, making it easier for him to slip in. Half the team had shifted to take on the hyenas, while the other half armed themselves against the hunters and Collectors.

Ben wanted to tear down the Johnston's Meat-Packaging sign the moment he saw it. Instead, he stayed low to the ground and out of sight until the attack began. He was close to the building, receiving information through the link as he went. The overgrown grass helped keep him hidden as he neared the back of the building.

The teams were almost ready when he heard a sound he never wanted to hear again in all of his lifetimes. A pain-filled roar. It felt as if a switch had flipped inside of him. His vision turned red, and he could feel his body changing, lengthening somehow. The last thing he consciously thought was that he had to get to his mate, and now.

***

Marie walked into a large, brightly lit room. Compared to the rest of this place, the room was damn near spotless. Another cage sat on the far side up against the back wall, with cables running from its bars across the floor and into a machine on the opposite side of the room. On closer inspection, she noticed the cage wasn't empty, a lone figure lay at the center of it.

She wanted to tear off the collar and slice these people to bits. The sight of the old warthog lying lifeless on the floor, discarded when he was no longer of use, drove a spike of rage into her body.

A single hunter walked over, and dragged the body out by his hoof. Marie watched as the shifter was tossed into a corner alongside tobacco guy. At least she thought it was him, since the body was in the same clothing he'd been wearing, but was now missing a head.

"Ah, there you are," Russo said as he walked in from the left. "Your turn to be of use to the cause. Take her to the cage."

Marie struggled and fought the movements of her own body, but in the end, she found herself standing in the center of the cage. Before she had a chance to realize what was happening, she heard a click, the collar was gone, and the cage was locked. She could move freely again, and the first thing she did was roar long and loud, before charging the bars.

"Don't waste your energy, bear. I've held much larger than you in there." Russo laughed and removed his coat jacket with a flourish any beauty queen would have been proud of. "Now, on with the show."

Where did this Collector come from? He wasn't acting like any demon she'd ever fought.

"I've seen that look before," Russo quipped. "Trust me, I'm all demon, simply version two point O. An upgrade from the standard model, new operating system—any way you look at it, I'm top dog around here."

Marie was surprised the bastard's head didn't explode with the size of his ego. She'd seen a few of the other Collectors in the zoo, and none of them behaved even remotely like this one.

"And you, my dear, are going to help me remain that way," he said while rolling up the sleeves of his white dress shirt to reveal the movie star's signature tattoos.

The crush of the bars against her body was nothing compared to the fury running through it. Russo pushed a few buttons on the small control panel in front of him, making the bars hum to life. She retreated to the center of the cage and watched the sparks of electricity arc from bar to bar. He was going to electrocute her? How was that going to help him?

"You see, I've discovered how useful shifters can be. Compared to humans, shifters contain an untapped resource, a more than sufficient life force, and the larger the animal, the more that can be harvested. Shifters live ten lifetimes to each human's one. Imagine now, if you could harness that energy, use it, mold it into whatever you wanted." He waved his hand up and down his body. "You can see how effective these *treatments* have been." He raised his arms, admiring them. "No sign of degeneration. Increased strength and vitality, and a longer life for the host. It's perfect."

Except for the part about sucking the life out of shifters to do it.

Russo unbuttoned his shirt and began attaching what looked like heart monitor leads to his chest, before sitting down in an overly cushioned chair.

His fingers circled a flashing green button as he carried on with his monologue. "There's a new world order shifter. We Collectors, like this side of the veil, and we've decided to stay. Instead of destroying this reality, we're going to repopulate and rebuild it to suit us. All you managed to do by releasing your friends was to extend their insignificant lives by a few months at most. They'll be rounded up and brought back to their fate." He raised his hand over the button. "I'm really going to enjoy this bear."

Pain. Instant and piercing. Her need to fight back was instinctual, and even if it wasn't, Marie refused not to at least try. The arcs of electricity flew from the steel bars and attached to her fur coat, leaving a white, pulsing effect encasing her body. She felt as if she was being pulled apart from the inside.

She could see Russo lounging back, with his hands behind his head, in his chair, as if he were having a spa treatment. Bastard. As the pressure spiked, she couldn't contain her pain-filled roar any longer, no matter what she did. It angered her even more, knowing that he would get a great deal of satisfaction from hearing it.

If there were even the slightest chance, Marie would end Russo's life, but she couldn't help but wonder, how many "Russo's" were actually out there?

***

The red faded from his vision, and his view of the world had changed. It seemed as if he'd been living his life looking through the noise of an old analog television. Now, it all seemed so clear. The world around him crackled with life, and he was finally a part of it.

He dug his claws into the damp earth and lunged forward, charging directly at the two hyena-shifters guarding an entrance.

It was time to get his mate back.

***

At first, Marie thought the flashing emergency lights were a side effect of whatever Russo was doing to her, but she soon realized they weren't when the Collector jumped up from his chair, ripped off the leads, and halted the machine.

Through the small windows, she could make out flashes of white light moments before explosions began ringing out around them. The gunfire came next, and Marie knew her rescuers had arrived in glorious style.

She watched with rapt attention as Russo began shouting out orders while gathering the leads, popping the control panel out of the machine, and stuffing it all into a silver backpack sitting on the desk. Marie knew she needed that piece of machinery if they ever had a chance of derailing the Collectors' plans.

The building shook, and Marie would have laughed if she had not been in her bear form. The goddesses were good and pissed.

"You think you've won some sort of victory here, foolish animal. You've stopped nothing," Russo yelled. "Now, I leave you to your fate, and perhaps our paths will cross again, bear."

Marie charged the cage door, again and again. She couldn't let the demon get away. Which only made him laugh harder while he collected his suit jacket.

A loud growl was the only warning as both Collectors and hyenas barreled into the room, followed by a bear. The biggest damn grizzly bear she'd ever seen. He was stunning.

"Marie."

"Ben?"

He quickly batted one of the hunters away, causing him to land only inches from her. Marie shifted and reached out for the keys on the man's belt, when suddenly the hunter sat up and grabbed hold of her hand.

"You looking for this, sweetie?" he hissed while holding out the key. If only all the hunters were as stupid as this one. Shifter strength came in handy.

With no effort at all, Marie crushed the bones in his hand with her own. "Thank you, yes it is." With her other hand, she plucked the key from the now screaming man, and sharply pulled him into the bars, breaking his neck.

She stood and fit the key into the lock, threw the door open, and shifted back into her bear. Marie dodged another flying hyena, and headed to the door she saw Russo slink out of.

"I'm going after the primary Collector. We need what's in the bag he's carrying," she explained to Ben, who'd built up an impressive pile of beheaded demons in front of him.

"I'll be right behind you, mate." Gods, she loved the sound of that word.

Marie sprinted through the door and down the corridor, passing shifters as she went, both rescuers and those freed. The place was in chaos, and she couldn't be happier to see their little operation coming to an end.

When she reached a T at the end of the corridor, she had to make a split-second decision, right or left.

Left.

The voice rang through her head, and she didn't question it. Her claws scraped along the concrete floor as she picked up speed. A single door was open on the right side, and she took it without breaking stride, coming out into a five-bay loading dock.

Cattle gates hung to one side, and ramps led down into what used to be refrigerated delivery trucks, now holding the remains of more dead shifters. She gagged at the smell, trying desperately not to throw up even though she didn't have any food in her stomach.

A small shift in the air was her warning, making her look up to find the back axle of another truck rolling over the edge of the equipment loft above. She closed her eyes and flexed for the impact. There was no time to get out of its path.

Another gust of wind followed by the sound of heavy crashing echoed off to her right. Marie opened her eyes to find Ben standing beside her, and the axel all the way across the loading docks.

His dark brown eyes softened when he looked down at her as she rubbed herself against her big bear.

"Thank you, love."

"Anytime."

"So there's two of you is there," Russo snarled. "Isn't that romantic, you can die together." He pulled out a handgun from behind his back and began firing.

Marie and Ben raced underneath the loft Russo was standing on. The bullets ricocheted through the drywall, barely missing them. There was nowhere for them to escape. If they ran out, they'd be shot, if they stayed where they were, they'd be shot.

Ben moved his body in front of her and pushed her back against the wall, protecting her with his own body. *"Why doesn't the Collector release the human body and make his escape?"*

"If he does that, he wouldn't be able to take the bag with him, and I get the feeling he's overly fond of this body."

Then she saw the solution.

"Mate, we need to push those poles over so that the loft will come crashing down, Russo and all."

"Done," Ben agreed before charging straight at the farthest one away while Marie took the pole closest.

With their big bear bodies and shifter strength, they leaned into the metal and began pushing. Bullets were raining down faster now. The timbers above her started to creak and groan loudly, before a sharp snapping sound gave them the sign to get out of the way.

She dove from underneath, landing against a wall of tires. Regaining her feet, Marie could see Ben safe on the other side of the collapsed loft. Scratching off to the other side caught her attention, and she went to investigate and found Russo attempting to crawl away with the backpack clutched in his hand.

Both of his legs stuck out at odd angles, while half of his movie star face had been sheared clean off, leaving only bone. Considering the host body was mostly dead when the Collector took it over, the injuries hadn't stopped him. The human was only a shell the demon inhabited.

When he reached for the gun lying a few inches away, Marie placed one of her massive paws on it. Ben used his teeth to rip the backpack out of the demon's hand and set it aside.

"Look what you've done to me. This body was perfect, now it's worthless," Russo screamed. "This isn't the end, bear, far from it."

Jake Russo, actor and heartthrob's, limp shell of a body slid to the ground as a translucent black ball of vapor poured from its eyes.

The Collector had abandoned his host and escaped straight through a cinderblock wall.

"Nooo." Even though she knew there was no way for her to stop him, Marie would need to be a goddess for that, she was still angry with herself for letting him go.

Ben came over and rubbed his big head against hers. *"We still managed to get you out, as well as many shifters. It's a good day in my book, and look, we still have this. What is it?"* Ben asked while nudging the backpack with his paw.

"Hopefully, something we can use to fight these creatures. Because if not, we may be fighting a losing battle."

Chapter Fourteen

Marie watched as Timothy and his parents left the restricted area hand in hand. They'd be taking up residence in the avian section of the bunkers, where there would be space to stretch their wings. Being present for moments like that made all the pain worth it. It'd been days since she'd returned to the bunkers, and every inch of her body still ached.

Due to her shifter metabolism, it wasn't typical to feel aches and pains after a few days of healing minor wounds. Nevertheless, she was flat on her back yet again. Jewel had checked her over twice, to make sure her findings were correct, and discovered that whatever Russo had done to her had actually killed many of the cells in her body. The good news, they would regenerate in time.

Ben had set up a large oval patio lounger in the center of the courtyard, so that she could rest and recuperate and not be shut up in their room

Ben's mother was still recovering in the infirmary. She'd undergone many more sessions with Russo before they'd rescued her. Once she was better, she'd have her own room here among them.

Over one hundred and forty shifters were saved from the two locations, and were settling in among the clan and pack. The alpha triads had already drawn up plans for an expansion to the bunker system to keep ahead of the growing need as the number of displaced shifters grew.

Of course, now that Ben was a full bear-shifter, they'd been offered a room among the clan, which they'd emphatically refused. Marie hadn't told her story to the clan, but more to the point, Ben couldn't wrap his mind around how anyone could blame her for anything, given what they knew about her family.

They'd decided, if they had to live underground, they wanted to live here, in the restricted area. No one argued them the point.

In the stranger things were happening category, when Joseph and Sarah had moved into the restricted area, a few brows were raised. The poor hyena-shifter had to be carried in, She was shaking too hard to walk on her own. At first, Marie had been confused by Joseph's reaction and protectiveness over the albino hyena, but seeing the way he looked at Sarah explained enough.

Not so long ago, she'd thought Joseph had been interested in the human-shifter that had arrived a week earlier. She was blonde, tall, and willowy, a classic beauty, however when Sarah had been found, that all changed. Most in their little community had welcomed Sarah warmly when she'd arrived.

Though the same thing couldn't be said about Raine's reaction. One look at the hyena, and she curled back her lip in disgust, shouting how another beast had moved in. Seriously, the woman wasn't endearing herself to anyone. Even the children avoided her as if she were contagious.

Even Ben, with his give-people-a-chance attitude, had had his fill of Raine.

As for Sarah, Marie wanted to help her somehow. She understood part of what the small hyena-shifter had been through, and hoped her experience and knowledge would give their newest arrival hope that better things were waiting for her.

Marie was considering going over to speak with the hyena when Ben came walking back into the courtyard. The handsome man spent more time in his bear form than human. The joy he felt in being one with his bear was felt by everyone, endearing him even further among the clan. He was in full share-the-love mode.

His unusually large size was still a mystery, though.

"Hello, mate, how are you feeling this afternoon?"

Ben was constantly checking in with her, which made Marie feel loved and cared for.

"I'm getting stronger every day," she replied. "I'll be back to my old self by this time next week."

"Don't push it. Remember, Jewel ordered you to relax."

Marie couldn't help but laugh. "Haven't we had this conversation before?"

Ben joined in her laughter before sitting down beside her. "Maybe this time around you'll even listen."

"Doubt it."

He set a familiar silver backpack down on the table in front of her lounger. She'd lost track of the device once the triads had received it. "Has anyone been able to figure out what that thing is?"

"Not yet," he explained. "A few components were broken during the fight."

"So, what now?"

"The triads have asked me to take a look at it, and see if I can figure any of it out. But I wanted to talk to you first."

Marie knew that Ben loved taking things apart down to their core pieces. "You wanted to talk to me?"

"Yeah. I realize the contents of this bag could be a trigger for you. A reminder of that time and the suffering you had to endure. If you don't want me to bring it into our personal space, I won't. I can work on it in the tools room, and you never have to see it again."

She took the time to think about it. Would the machine that helped kill so many shifters make her uncomfortable in their home? Absolutely. Was it enough for her to stand in the way of her mate figuring out what it was, and how they could fight against it in their home? No.

"You can keep it here, mate. I want to find a way to stop them from ever being able to use that technology against us again."

Marie had gone back into the room where she'd been placed in the cage to search for the collar that had rendered her incapable of moving without permission, but it was gone. She'd hoped they could have torn that apart as well, to find a way to deactivate it, but they'd lost their chance.

Ben crawled closer onto the oversized lounger and lay down beside her. She could remember a time not too long ago when she would have fought against any and all affection directed at her. Now she willingly curled into her mate's welcoming arms, safe in the knowledge that love wasn't a fantasy, and that she was deserving of it.

Not bad for a once dishonored bear.

ABOUT THE AUTHOR

Lilli Carlisle lives in the country near Toronto, Canada. She is the mother of two wonderful girls, wife to an amazing man, and servant to the pets in her life, and she's a member of Toronto Romance Writers. Lilli writes paranormal romance, and believes love should be celebrated and shared. After all, everybody needs a little romance, excitement, intrigue, and passion in their lives.

Connect with Lilli:
Instagram:/lillicarlisle
facebook.com/lillicarlisleauthor
twitter.com/LilliCarlisle

www.BOROUGHSPUBLISHINGGROUP.com

If you enjoyed this book, please write a review. Our authors appreciate the feedback, and it helps future readers find books they love. We welcome your comments and invite you to send them to info@boroughspublishinggroup.com. Follow us on Facebook, Twitter and Instagram, and be sure to sign up for our newsletter for surprises and new releases from your favorite authors.

Are you an aspiring writer? Check out www.boroughspublishinggroup.com/submit and see if we can help you make your dreams come true.